# QUICK-TRIGGER COUNTRY

Turk was just a kid when he hooked up with Curly Bill Graham's outlaw gang, but he quickly made a name for himself as a fast and fearless gunslinger. Membership of the Graham gang brought Turk the excitement he'd always craved—until the border raids turned into an excuse for senseless killing. When Graham's crew slaughtered a band of unarmed Mexicans, Turk drew the line.

When range war flared, Turk and the Graham gang were on opposite sides. He'd fight to the death to get back on the law's side, but if he wound up on Boot Hill, he'd take Curly Bill with him!

# QUICK-TRIGGER COUNTRY

## Nelson Nye

GUNSMOKE

First published by Mills and Boon

This hardback edition 2004
by BBC Audiobooks Ltd
by arrangement with
Golden West Literary Agency

ISBN 0 7540 8261 X

**British Library Cataloguing in Publication Data available.**

Printed and bound in Great Britain by
Antony Rowe Ltd., Chippenham, Wiltshire

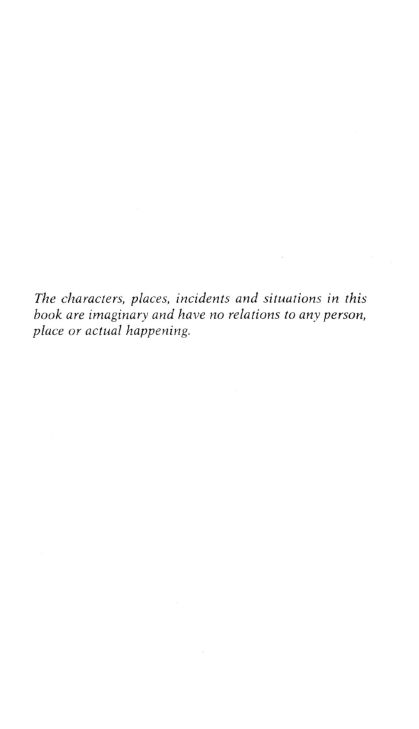

# ONE

Old "I Personally" Ruebusch, resident manager of the biggest cattle outfit in the Tombstone end of the Territory, packed his lower lip with snuff and, creaking comfortably back in his swivel, ran a disparaging stare over this latest addition to the Roman 4 crew. The youngster, in part because of the color of his hair but mostly because of his chip-on-shoulder attitude, was known by the sobriquet of Turkey Red and was down by that name on the timesheet.

The manager, who had never been caught in a generous impulse, gave him plenty of time to get rid of his assurance. For a wagon train stray who couldn't remember his own folks, the kid figured to be doing pretty well for himself since spreading his blankets on a Roman 4 bunk. He'd been accorded a certain brusque deference because of his demonstrated speed with a pistol and this had naturally led him mistakenly to assume himself a man among men, a concept he appeared to value and an illusion which had upon occasion caused him to act a whopping fool. All of which Ruebusch was pleasantly aware of. "Like it here, do you?"

The kid, rolling down the off corner of his mouth, allowed that it would do. He hooked both thumbs in his cartridge belt and scrinched his eyes with a hint of impatience.

"You look almighty young," Ruebusch said.

The kid's chin came up with an affronted glare. a regular ape, Ruebusch scornfully thought, reminded of the man the kid took for his model. He hooked out a drawer with the ease of long practice and hoisted the bottle-glass shine of his boots. "We spend half our profits building up a tough crew and every time a job comes up needing half a gram of savvy every qualified hand on the place is off somewhere."

While he gave this a chance to get properly sunk in, Ruebusch hiked his cold stare from the kid's scuffed boots to the cocky slant of his sweat darkened stetson. A prize sap, Ruebusch thought, letting it show through his expression. A brand for the burning if he had ever clapped eyes on one. Wouldn't top the scales at 120 with his boots on— including those special built-up heels by which he hoped to appear taller than his actual five foot five.

"How old are you, Turkey?"

Resentful color crept above the open top of the kid's shirt collar. "Old enough to earn what you're payin' me."

Ruebusch said, "You ever been shot at?"

He watched the kid's blue eyes narrow. Red understood where the talk was being hazed, but like he wanted it out in the open he said, "If it's

8

Fanshaw that's bothering you I can have him off that crick before another sun gits up."

Ruebusch worked his jaws around and spat. "Don't see what you could do that Strehl and Buck ain't tried already."

Buck Linderstrom was the Roman 4 ramrod and, like Ruebusch himself, had stock in the company. Strehl was a boot licking straw boss who'd already shown signs of having it in for the new hand.

Ruebusch, still eyeing him disparagingly, said: "I personally couldn't afford to send a boy on a chore grown men is scared to tackle. I'll ride in tomorrow and hash it over with Wyatt Earp."

He waved Red toward the door, smugly pleased when the kid proved his estimate right by stubbornly refusing to move from his tracks. "What you need for this chore," Turkey Red growled, "is guts. And I've got 'em."

Ruebusch snorted. "I never measure guts by the size of a fellow's lip. You stay away from that place. Instead of ramming around like a two-bit copy of that damned Curly Bill, if you want folks to think you're big as you figure you better go scrape that fuzz off your mug!"

She was Ruebusch's wife and Red had kept that in mind for the whole two months he had been with this outfit. Holly was her name and even when, increasingly, he'd been singled out to ride with her he hadn't allowed this intimacy to suck him into any open disregard of the trust implied by the privilege. This was a big unsettled country and there were a lot of tough hombres riding through these hills; his skill with a pistol was what had earned this preference. Red had never doubted it. And yet, sometimes he'd got some awful queer notions and it had taken a deal of will power to remind himself that she was a married woman, just impulsive and uncommon friendly. She didn't mean nothing by it. Just her way—a little skittish, maybe, but that was understandable in a girl scarce turned eighteen.

Buck Linderstrom had told him off to reset a number of posts that had got loosened during the bronc stomper's work in the breaking pen recently. The morning was half shot by the time he had got finished and Linderstrom had told him to ride over to Willow Springs and see what-all was needed to put the line shack there into shape for winter use. It was a good seven miles from headquarters and he hadn't covered two when Holly came riding up and allowed she would go along with him.

"Mister Ruebusch know about this?" Red said.

She gave him one of those long slow stares and let him see the quick flash of her teeth. With that honey colored hair she sure made a picture. "He doesn't know I'm around half the time," she answered, scornful. "Always up to his ears in those accounts. Come on, I'll beat you to that catclaw thicket!"

She was off like the dust sifting out of a twister but he got there ahead of her without half trying. High Sailin Brown—that was his own private horse—was one of the fastest hides to ever come out of Texas, a Billy he'd got off a saddleblanket gambler who had waited too long after laying down his character. The horse looked pudding-footed but could run like a Neuches steer.

She came up out of breath, eyes bright and hair flying. He watched her tucking the strands back in place and caught himself wondering what she'd do if he grabbed and kissed her. It got him pretty steamed up and downright shamed and riled besides. "You better be gettin' on back," he growled. "I'm like to be gone the best part of the day and Mister Ruebusch—"

"Fiddlesticks!" Her eyes came up at him through the shine of her lashes. "What's the matter with you, Turk?"

"Ain't nothin' the matter with *me*," he scowled, recalling that scene with the manager last evening and thinking thoughts that were best put plumb out of his mind.

She was watching him curiously with head tipped back and her eyes getting darker and her chin more pronounced like it almost always seemed to when things didn't shape to her liking. "If I didn't know you better I would think you didn't want me."

He didn't try to figure that out. He said gruffly: "I got work to do."

"You're not expecting to work all the way down and back are you?"

He scowled at High Sailin's ears. "It don't look right," he said, "you traipsin' off with me every time I—" and let the rest of it go with his ears getting red.

Her cheeks turned a little stiff, and then her lips pulled back. "You thinking of Ruebusch?" She

11

laughed. "He thinks you're part of the scenery."

His teeth grated together and she leaned nearer, putting a hand on his arm. "I wasn't trying to bemean you, Turk. It's just that what you said was so . . . so *ridiculous.*" Then her eyes showed rebellion. "It's true enough though—about Rue-busch, I mean. All he thinks about is figures—"

"He sure knows how to pick 'em!"

Red shouldn't have spoke like that and he knew it; it had kind of slipped out in the bitterness of his resentment. And he wouldn't have been surprised if she had really torn into him.

She looked more astonished than anything, astonished and halfway pleased, he thought, startled. She dragged a deep breath away down into the inside of her and the bulges of her shirt-waist shaped more provocative than ever. It didn't seem to Red that she had very much on under it.

The way she twisted her face around, looking up at him, had something different about it, something strange, almost . . . exciting. "Do you really think so, Turk?"

She was watching him with her bright eyes half shut. His heart got to banging. Her horse fetched her nearer. He tore his stare away from her. He didn't want to do anything foolish.

He said in a kind of half strangled way, "It's time I was gettin' over there," and ribbed his horse with a heel. She ribbed hers too. He didn't say any more about not wanting her with him.

They rode perhaps three miles without either of them breaking the country's deep silence. Red kept his stare on the gullied slopes ahead of them but he could feel the looks she kept turning in his direction. They came up onto a bench and he could see the green tops of the trees at Willow Springs and an edge of the shack showing gray through the branches.

"Turk—" She reined her horse closer. He saw her hand reached out and felt the grip of fingers, felt it tighten on his arm. "You don't know what it's like being married to a man old enough to be your father."

Red kept his eyes on the shack.

After a moment she took her hand away. Her walking horse sidled nearer and their knees came together and rubbed to the rhythmic motion and he felt sweat crack through the pores of his skin and it was all he could do to keep his mind on his business.

She said, "I've got the whole of my life still ahead of me, Turk. I want to live it, not be shut up in a monastery!"

Red's thoughts plunged around like a bronc with the hobbles on.

"I know. I married him. I thought we'd travel," she said bitterly. "I didn't know I was going to be buried in this godforsaken place. He treats the furniture better—at least he uses it! I don't see what I ever—"

Her voice choked up. She reined her horse away from him.

"You won't ever have to go hungry," he said.

She did pretty near fly into him then. "There are hungers more cruel than going without eating."

They'd come up to the springs. "You better try it sometime," he said, swinging down. He could have told her plenty about going without eating.

He led High Sailin off into the trees. He found a place where there was some lush looking grass, loosened the cinch and took off the bridle. Told Holly she'd better let her pony feed too and took a look at his shadow. Going on for twelve o'clock. He went up to the shack.

It could stand some going over. Didn't look like it had even been slept in since the outfit had wangled this range off Tadpole. He'd been riding for old man Glover then, combing brush-splitters out of the San Pedro for him.

He pushed open the door. Rats had got at what grub had been left here. A big sack of beans was scattered all over and the left wall bunk could do with new slats. A lid was gone off the stove and water stains showed where the roof had been leaking. Probably take a full day to get the place fixed up. Have to fetch out some boards and . . .

But his mind wasn't on it. He kept remembering the way she had looked at him and the scent of her nearness, and Ruebusch thinking he was part of the scenery.

Calling up Ruebusch didn't help him much now. He could hear her moving around outside, humming a little, tapping the leg of a boot with her crop. And a fluttery trembling crept up through his stomach as he recalled the feel of her leg brushing his. He looked around the shack wildly. The thing to do, he knew, was get the hell out of here. He was heading for the door when he heard her scream.

He dived out of that shack like hot grease from a skillet. She wasn't in sight. Both horses had their heads up, ears pricked forward, staring in a direction where the willow screen bulked heaviest. He ran toward it, not forgetting he was riding for a tough and brutal outfit. He didn't know what he expected to see—Apaches, maybe, or some of the fellows this spread had done dirt to. He had his gun up and ready when he plunged through the trees.

He saw the springs and the stock trampled mud around the edges of them and for a couple of heartbeats that was all he did see. No Indians, no outlaws, no dispossessed ranchers. Just the springs and the willows and the sun beating through them throwing up little flashes off the leaves and the water. Then he gave a sudden start and slipped his gun back into leather.

She was face down in the weeds about six feet to the left of the water. Motionless and crumpled.

He stared with the breath piled up in his throat. He had to swallow three times before he could get enough air to breathe with.

His eyes raked the clearing without finding anything to explain what had happened. His ears couldn't catch any sound of departure. He moved nearer studying the ground all about her. No loose rock. No sign of a struggle. She lay with one arm doubled under her, one leg drawn up and her disarrayed skirt hiked over the knee of the other.

He got her turned over. There was an earth stained place on her forehead where her face had been in the dirt. She didn't look too pale but there wasn't much breath going in and out of her.

Picking her up with great care, and bad worried, he moved through the trees. The scent of her hair, the clean woman smell of her, did nothing to calm the jumbled whirl of his thoughts. He put her down on the grass in a patch of blue shadow and felt uncommonly helpless.

With this sense of inadequacy heavily riding him he was turning to go dip up a hatful of water when a groan came out of her. He wheeled back to peer down at her. Her lips faintly trembled.

She moaned again as he bent over her, abruptly flexing an arm. Her eyes came open. Wild as a stallion bronc's they looked. She snatched her legs up under her and came half onto an elbow before she saw him and sank back, shaking.

"Sho," he said, dropping down beside her, "you'll be all right now. What happened?"

"That awful snake! Oh, Turk—" she moaned. She flung both arms around his neck and clung to him sobbing like a frightened child. "There, there," he soothed, "you're all right now."

"But it hurts so, Turk—"

"My God! Did the damn thing strike you?" He pulled loose and reared back, getting hold of his gotching knife. "Quick! I better—where'd it git you?"

She blinked tear streaked lashes, swallowed a couple of times hard and shuddered. "It . . . it was my ankle, I think."

"Well, get off it," he said, "and let's have a look at it. Which ankle is it?"

"The right one." Her fingers kept nervously picking at her skirt but she pushed out the foot with a little whimper of pain. "Do . . . do you suppose I—Is it swollen much?"

"I can't tell with your skirt over it that way."

She looked flustered, cheeks coloring, but

pulled it up a short inch. "Can't you . . . sort of tell by feeling?"

"I can't feel nothin' through that boot!"

She lay back on her elbows. "I guess you'll have to pull it off."

He was careful as he could be but it didn't come easy. He was tempted to slit the leather with his knife but she shook her head. "Just pull a little harder."

Sweat rolled off his chin. He kept tugging. Her eyes were closed tight. She never let out a peep. Not even when her skirt fell back. He reckoned she'd passed out but she hadn't. "That stockin'," he said, looking dubious. With her eyes still shut she reached up under her.

"You can pull it down now."

He looked the ankle all over, and it was something to look at, but he couldn't find any punctures. "You sure this is the one?"

"Oh, yes!" she cried, wincing. "It feels just as though it was *broken.*"

It wasn't broken. It didn't look to him like it was much swollen either. He felt it over carefully. "Must of wrenched it," he muttered, "when you jumped clear of that snake. Here, see if you can stand."

She smoothed down her skirt and gathered the hurt leg under her. He gave her a hand and she came up but sagged into him. "Oh-h!" she cried, trembling. She got her free hand hooked around his belt and breathed deeply. "Are you sure it's not broken?"

"Try wigglin' it," he said.

She took the hand away from his belt and put

the arm around his shoulder, letting him feel the softness of her. And that was when, glancing down, he saw more than either of them had figured on. Someway, getting up, the neck of her waist had come unfastened.

There was a fluttering in his knee joints. His ears felt hot. She said, "I can't—I know I can't. If you will help me get to the cabin, Turk . . . Do you suppose you could carry me? My head's just whirling around something awful."

There was sweat on Turk's face and a cyclone inside him as he picked her up and started for the shack. Her head came against his shoulder, the soft mass of her hair pushed against his cheek. His grip suddenly tightened.

He kicked the door shut with his heel.

# TWO

HE FELT LIKE a treacherous dog when he got the door wrenched open and they came out of the shack into the yard's bright glare. He looked at the willows with their green leaves hot and still and at the patches of brassy sky showing through them and at the horses off yonder still cropping at the grass, and was surprised in his shame to find the world had not collapsed. He would have pulled away from her in a nausea of revulsion but she was too wise to let him. She clung to him tightly. "You mustn't blame yourself, Turk—we couldn't help it. You know we couldn't. Don't worry. No one will ever guess." Over and over she kept reassuring him softly, pressing herself against him, until his chin came up a little and his arm finally tightened around her slim waist.

She settled more heavily against him then. She even managed a wavery smile. "After all," she said with an attempt at lightness, "the sky hasn't fallen."

"But Ruebusch . . ." Turk scowled.

She pushed back against his arm. "You can't think I'd be fool enough to tell!"

"It ain't that." He frowned at her bare foot, trying to pull his thoughts together. "I'll get a job someplace—"

"You're not thinking of leaving!"

"We'll both leave," he said. "You can't go back to him now. First place, I wouldn't let you—"

"Let me! Are you crazy?"

He stared at her blankly. In the jumbled whirl of his own emotions he found it difficult to concentrate, impossible to achieve any real degree of coherency, and naturally assumed her own condition no less chaotic. "We'll make out all right. Quick as I can git a little money put by we'll start a herd of our own. Have . . ."

He caught the look of her then, the glassy brightness of her regard. He saw the edge of one lip crawling off her white teeth. "You think I'd run off and live with you in a shack on a shoestring?"

"It won't be that bad. I've got a rep. I'll git work—"

"You *are* a greenie!" Scorn flashed through her glance and she twisted out of his arm and stood away from him, angry. She pushed the yellow hair back out of her eyes. "Things are bad enough now without—Sometimes I think you're impossible!"

He tromped hard on his temper. He made allowances for her. "We got to look at this sensible. When two people's in love—"

She laughed then, threw back her head and laughed like a loony. "Love!" She wiped her eyes on her shirtwaist, still shaking with a kind of hysteria. Her voice railed out at him. "You think

I'd throw over all I've got as his wife to run off with a kid that isn't dry behind the ears? There are a lot of things I *haven't* got but give me credit, anyway, for more intelligence than that!"

Turk gaped at her dumbly. There was a roaring in his ears and he could feel the leak of sweat between his shoulders and he was recollecting now how it had been around here before Roman 4 had offered him twenty more on the month than he'd been getting from old man Glover. She'd been doing her riding with Linderstrom then and it seemed to him abruptly he'd been as big a chump as Ruebusch.

A swirling haze blotted out the mocking curl of her lips and he moved a step or two toward her blindly, the fingers of his hands becoming stiff as flexing talons. Then the haze thinned away and he could see her again.

The scorn was gone from her now, dissolved and washed away in fright. Her eyes looked like they would burst from their moorings and she was pale as he'd ever seen her. She stood as though frozen with a hand up in front of her, but he had hold of himself now and blackly turned away from her. spurs jangling harshly as he strode to High Sailin.

He snatched the bridle off the horn and rammed the bit in the gelding's mouth and, bending, yanked the slack from the cinch and got bitterly into the saddle. He stopped then, turning for another black look at her.

She wasn't paying him any mind now and the color was back in her cheeks again, her mouth almost ugly in the clamp of her lips. He watched her pull on her stocking, stamp into her boot and go off through the willows in the direction of the springs. Pretty soon she came back, slamming into her saddle. She had left the horse bridled but she had to get down again to tighten the cinches, and he let her. Let her lead off too, silently swinging in behind her.

They got practically in sight of the ranch without speaking. Turk, during those miles, rode prey to his tumultuous emotions. Shame and the flare of resentment and, behind these, the heat of the steadily building fury shook him by turns and left him incapable of an approach to calm reasoning.

At first his thoughts had shrunk away from the magnitude of what had transpired in that shack at the line camp, but finally he had looked at his guilt and accepted it. What was done was done and it seemed to him now that all along he must have sensed in their growing intimacy that these continuing contacts must result in what had happened. Right there, without realizing, he glimpsed a part of the pattern, but his mind was too full of other things either to follow it further or track it back to its obvious source.

Holly's jibs still rankled, still cut at him like whips, and the scorn of Ruebusch yesterday came back to feed his resentment and fan even brighter the sorrel flames of his mounting fury. And yet, by some grim alchemy of associations beyond his grasp to fathom, the girl had got into his blood. In spite of everything he still wanted her. He could not see her as she was but only as she had seemed to him, and the ecstacy of that moment returned again and again to fan the sparks of his anger.

He left her two miles short of headquarters, turning aside without a word, sending High Sailin obliquely off through the brush. He would show her, by God! He would show Ruebusch, too! If it was the last thing he did!

He reined the big brown toward the Whetstones. He could see their slopes blue and purple in the distance above the tawny shimmer of the surrounding sunbaked range. Fanshaw's place lay over against those slopes and, though he didn't expect to run into any Apaches, he didn't aim to be caught napping. This was gun-packing country with the law mostly served from a cutaway holster and the one that got it bellering first was generally given the verdict.

It was a violent land, yet even so lead poisoning, as Turk saw it, was something a fellow usually had to contract. And the ones that got down with it mostly had it coming—like that crazy damned Fanshaw with his jaw stuck out around that buffalo gun.

He had settled five-six years before with a piddling jag of longhorned cattle on a spring that came out of the south flank of the Whetstones. He never owned one inch of land; Roman 4 held title to some of it.

Roundtank Springs fed an all-year creek that watered twenty miles of Ruebusch's best grazing, the only drink his stock could conveniently get without they browsed clear east to the San Pedro. Willow Springs was good enough but the range had been overgrazed and there was stock along the San Pedro that belonged to hostile outfits. Since Fanshaw had been in the country first Ruebusch had tried to put up with it, taking his sass and breeding his cows for him.

They figured now it was a mistake.

Roman 4, owned by Eastern capital, was a big operation. Too big, Turk thought, to be getting stewed up over one old mossback and a jag of crossbred cattle. But it looked like bigness could get to be a kind of a disease, and Ruebusch and Linderstrom had halfway got to viewing themselves as a second Murphy-Dolan when Fanshaw damned the creek up. He hadn't opened his mouth. Just put in a charge where the water spilled through the notch below his place and closed off the whole stream. It would spill over some time but Ruebusch needed it now.

A couple of weeks had gone past before he got wind of it. He lit into Linderstrom. Linderstrom got onto his horse and rode over to throw the fear into Fanshaw. This, at any rate, was how Turk had got it, but Fanshaw's old Sharps spoke louder than Linderstrom. He'd gone back three nights later and got run off again. Next time he'd sent Strehl with half the Roman 4 crew and the creek was still dry where the Roman 4 grazed it. There was Roman 4 cattle piled up all along Fanshaw's fenceline.

Turk reckoned this was a job cut to order.

The first gray light of approaching dawn was thrusting timid fingers up into the eastern blackness by the time Turk got back to the place where he'd parted with Holly. There was a wind scooting down off the higher bluffs, larruping his face with its lifted grit. It was raw enough to hunch a man's

24

shoulders and Turk had his wipe pulled up across his nose, chin settled deep into the threadbare collar of the brush jacket he'd had lashed on behind his saddle.

He wasn't really paying much attention to the weather, his mind being occupied with things more satisfactory. Off ahead a couple of miles at Roman 4 headquarters the lamps would be pushing yellow shafts through the thinning gloom; and the crew, breakfasts downed with scalding cups of black Arbuckle, would be catching up their mounts to get about the long day's riding.

He dragged the wipe off his face as he rode up toward the gate and brought his chin up out of the collar of his jacket. He wasn't expecting there'd be many hands around this late but what there were he figured to have known there was one fellow on this Roman 4 payroll that, by God, could get the job done.

Old Pablo was in the corral with his milk pails, Emilio helping him. Turk saw Pablo twist his head and stare a long moment before settling back to his work. Emilio cursed and blew on his fingers, regained his hold on the horns and hunched bony shoulders.

Turk didn't care whether they spoke to him or not. They'd chum up all right when the news got around. He felt seven foot tall riding through the gate hugging the prospect these next minutes would unfold. The prospect of him being accorded a man's due.

The fragrance of wood smoke was a strong homey smell in the rawness of the morning. The cavvy—the band of saddle stock—in the horse trap stood and watched him solemnly, and he looked at the animals a second time with the first faint stirring of unease. There hadn't ought to be near so many. He saw Parins with folded arms in the open door of the cook shack and wind pulled a waterfall sound from the tossing branches of the cottonwoods.

Turk looked at Parins. "Be over in a minute," he called with a wave.

The cook didn't move. He didn't say anything either. Turk latched onto something else then, the reason for the trap full of horses. The crew hadn't left! Four or five of the outfit hunkered on their boot-heels by the side of the bunkhouse. Another still shape was back of a window in the harness shed and three other men were watching from a corner of the barn.

The winkless stares of that silent crew at a time when those men would not normally have been here was unexpectedly something Turk had not counted on, but he shrugged it aside and swung down before the house. The day was too far advanced for the need of a lamp though one still spread its pale effulgence against the window of Ruebusch's office.

Turk had lived with this moment all the way back from Fanshaw's and would not be put off stride by such trifles. He couldn't still the pounding thump of his heart but he went up the steps with a display of nonchalance that would not have shamed the god of his deportment, Curly Bill, himself. He was reaching for the door to the manager's office when it opened. "Come in,"

Linderstrom said, stepping aside to give him room.

Ruebusch was back of his desk. "Sit down, Turkey."

It was the first time the manager had ever made such a courteous gesture. Something clicked far back on the edge of Turk's emotions and his glance, sweeping around, picked up the shape against the left wall. It had a face like a nutcracker —all nose and chin. This was Strehl, the pet gun hand. And behind Turk was Linderstrom. Ignoring the chair Turk moved a little to the right, watching the manager pack snuff against the front of his lower denture.

In a way Turk felt a little sorry for the bastard.

"Where you been?" Ruebusch said.

"Over to Fanshaw's lookin' out for your interests. Doin' what the rest of these yaps hadn't the guts to."

There was a growl from the left and Strehl's hand started hipward. "Go ahead," Turk sneered. "Go ahead and drag it."

A kind of wheeze racked Strehl's breathing but he let the hand fall away.

Linderstrom grinned.

The old man was furious. "Am I to understand you went over there after I personally told you to keep away from Fanshaw?"

"You been tryin' to git him—"

"Just a minute, Turk." That was Linderstrom. "Suppose you tell us what happened."

Strehl said with a snarl, "What the hell you think happened! He got run off same as—"

Turk was starting for Strehl when Linderstrom grabbed him. Ruebusch yelled, "You're fired! Get off my ranch!"

Turk stared at him, thunderstruck. He couldn't believe he had heard the man right. His ears got hot and a quiver got into his knee joints and a kind of red fog rolled up out of the corners until all he could see was the old man's apoplectic face.

Ruebusch was shrunk so far back in his swivel another inch would have turned the chair over when Turk became aware of Linderstrom's fingers. They were sunk into his left shoulder like the fangs of a wolf and there was a gun dug into the middle of Turk's back. "Take it easy, kid," the ramrod said, easing him carefully back away from the desk. "I've got ten men outside just bustin' to take a crack at you. You better keep that in mind if you aim to come out of this all in one piece."

He relaxed his grip and stepped back but kept his gun up. "Now suppose you tell us what went on over there."

Bootsteps banged across the boards of the porch. The door flew open. A dust covered rider stuck his face in. "Boss, there's water in . . ." He saw Linderstrom's gun and his jaw sagged.

Linderstrom shook Turk's shoulder. "You blow that dam?"

"Sure," Turk said. "I told you I'd took care of . . ."

"What about Fanshaw? Where was he when you were—"

"The little son of a bitch has killed him!" Ruebusch pounded the desk with his fists. "I won't be responsible—I call you boys to witness!

You heard me tell this wheyfaced pup to stay away from there!"

Strehl's nutcracker face came apart in a grin.

Linderstrom prodded Turk with his pistol. "Outside," he said and, when they hit the porch. "I'm afraid you're up against it, Turkey. By rights we ought to turn you over to Wyatt Earp but damn if I can sell a man that's et my grub down the river." He gave Turk a push. "Get aboard that bronc and punch a hole through the breeze."

# THREE

IT TOOK HIM two weeks to get to Tucson and he was still plenty riled when he got there. He guessed, in a way, he'd had it coming but that didn't make it any easier to take. He'd been put on and took off like a sheepherder's coat, first by Holly and then I Personally and he wasn't far from convinced the two were all of a piece.

One thing he was sure of. They'd had to get Fanshaw off that creek and, thanks to him, they had got him off—got his range and his buildings and his damned wall-eyed cattle! And the Roman 4 was a big enough outfit that when Wyatt Earp (who packed the tin in that country) got to sniffing around, all he'd ever catch wind of was a gent called Turkey Red. He'd been whipsawed like a greenie—like the very kid she'd named him!

Turk writhed every time he thought of it, clenching fists in a bitter fury each time his mind called up the steps by which, coldbloodedly, the Roman 4 bosses had set out to make a catspaw of him . . . the snide remarks and grins, the skeptical laughter. They had played him like a fish on a line.

But they couldn't have gotten away with it so cute if he hadn't inadvertently done most of the ground work, trying so desperately to impress them with an importance he'd no right to lay claim to.

He saw plain enough now that he'd been shoved on the dodge by his own tomfoolery, reaping the harvest his own duplicity had planted; for the hell of it was he hadn't killed that damned squatter. The obstreperous old stinker had tripped over his own rifle and just about blown the whole bottom of his face off—but try and get Earp to believe that now!

He put up at Levin's which faced west on Main between Pennington and Ott, because it was handy to the stages and therefore to the news. He didn't hear anything though about Fanshaw's killing and after a couple of nights, having run out of cash, he headed for Silver Lake.

This was a body of water on the Santa Cruz River roughly two miles south of town. It furnished, among other things, power for a flour mill; the main other thing being a two-floor hotel which was gathering a reputation for some pretty wild goings-on.

He got a job as the barkeep's third assistant—two bucks a night plus grub and stable privileges. From ten till along about three in the morning that place was a gold mine. Tucson was doing a lot of bragging about its "culture" but when the nabobs came to Silver Lake with their women Turk didn't see much difference between them and the customers of Bob Hatch's dive back in Tombstone.

The tavern faced east across the lake with the

Tucson Mountains back of it and a gallery across the front with great tall posts that ran clean up to the eaves. There was a railed-in balcony anchored to these posts where the girls the place furnished could take the air on sultry evenings. It could only be got onto from those little second floor rooms, which was where the girls did business. A flossy bunch with little signs on their doors like *France, Portugal, China, Argentina, Peru* and others too queer sounding for Turk to remember. These females cost the management three bucks a night to help kid the customers they were enjoying the life of Reilly.

The first floor was mostly given over to the bar and gambling rigs though there was another brace of cubicles at the back which were rented to sports who had brought their own fun. The sixth night after Turk got his job the boss called him into his office.

"You look like you got a head on your shoulders. Flack's been too sick. Think you could handle this job for the evening?"

Flack was one of the bouncers though at Silver Lake he had a more refined title. "All you've got to do," the boss said, "is perambulate around and keep your eyes skinned."

"Skinned for what?"

"Ha, ha," the boss grinned. He rolled the cigar across his gold inlay. "Ever worked in a place like this before?"

Turk shook his head. "I been punchin' cattle."

The boss nodded. "Guy that can handle cattle won't have no trouble with the kind of trade I get." He put a pair of brass knuckles and a sock on his

32

desk. "Busted heads is cheaper than a bunch of broke-up furniture. There'll be a fiver in it for you. Anyone starts to raise hell you take care of him. Quick."

Turk put the stuff in his pocket. "I'm stony," he said. "How about a little dough?"

The boss glanced in the book and shoved across his five nights' wages. "You can't wear those duds. See Arch—he'll fix you up."

Arch did. Like a man in a dream Turk caught the string tie and white shirt, the black cutaway and trousers and, when he got into them, felt like a monkey. Arch had to fix the tie for him. He was some surprised when he met himself in the mirror. He didn't look near as foolish as he'd imagined. He'd have passed in Tombstone for a regular high roller. "Your color's a little rugged," Arch said critically, "but considering your size, that might be an asset."

"What the devil's this sock for?" Turk asked, holding it out.

Arch looked at him and grunted. He took the sock and, going to a bucket, thrust a handful of sand into it, smacked it on his leg a couple of times and handed it back. "One of them clowns gets rough you wrap it around his noggin. Now get rolling and keep your eye peeled."

It was early yet. Things didn't generally get into full swing until the hands of the clock got to crowding midnight. The bar when Turk stepped into it was practically deserted. There were a couple of dudes shooting the breeze in a corner and one of the girls from upstairs held down a table with a glass of pale tea. Turk thought she was the one from Timbuktu, though if he'd seen her anywhere else he would have taken her for a Yaqui.

A well dressed gent who looked about half crocked hung against the bar with a watch on one fist shooting the breeze with one of the barkeeps. And one other fellow, a big guy rigged like a rancher, had a foot on the rail. Turk eyed this one morosely with his thoughts irrevocably prowling back to the Roman 4.

He went outside and rolled a smoke. It didn't give him much satisfaction. Despite all the figuring he had done, and all the pent-up wrath and bitterness, he still knew deep inside him there'd never be another to fill the place he'd given Holly. He called himself a fool but it don't change anything really. She'd got into his blood and that was all there was to it; no amount of soul searching or barbed prods from his pride could drive away the things she stirred in him.

He pitched his smoke into the night and went back.

The man in rancher's garb still had his foot on the rail. There was something about him that kept dragging Turk's glance around. Big enough, he looked, to hunt bears with a switch. Turk kept thinking he might catch a look at his face but the way the man was standing the glass didn't show it. His hair was black beneath the white ten-gallon stet-hat and he had broad shoulders—almost broad as Curly Bill, Turk, thought, his eyes abruptly narrowing. Behind the fancy shirt and pinto vest and the black-and-white checks that hugged his legs like skin, the man's shape was enough like Bill's to . . .

Turk sucked in his breath. The man had turned his face to say something to the barkeep, and that profile—by God, it *was* Curly Bill! Curly Bill at Silver Lake!

Turk, astounded, moved across to an empty table where a deck of cards lay open and, dropping into a chair, began to lay out a start in Klondyke the way he'd watched the house men do when they were waiting around. Over the cards he watched the big man at the bar.

Curly Bill around Tombstone was a name to conjure with. He was dark and ruggedly handsome and Turk saw the Yaqui setting out bait and thought to himself she might as well cut stick. This was too big a gent to waste his time on the likes of her. He must have felt the pull of Turk's stare for his head tipped up and his black eyes rummaged Turk's face in the gleam and shine of the back bar mirror.

Turk, flushing a little, dropped the stare to his cards, putting the jack of spades on top of the king of hearts. A voice at his shoulder pointed out the mistake, and Turk's swiveled glance found the Yaqui from Timbuktu leering down at him. "Oo is these man?" she asked in a husky whisper.

Turk swept the cards in a heap and got out of his chair, nettled as much by her interest as by the cheap perfume with which her presence enveloped him. He brushed past her brusquely heading for the door.

The midnight sky was filled with white fluffy

clouds. A breeze off the lake brought a rank smell of shore and yonder, across the dappled blue and silver of the intervening range, the lamps of Tucson gleamed like cats' eyes. He was not sur· prised at the big man's lack of recognition; always he had worshipped Curly Bill from afar, his attempted emulation the sincerest form of flattery. A mouse tiptoeing after an elephant.

But even a mouse might aspire to be large, Turk reflected morosely. It was hard to put into words how he felt about Bill. The man cast a whale of a shadow. Everything he did was bold, assured and confident. The country spoke of him in whispers and there were two schools of thought: one considering him a godsend, the champion of the ranch crowd; the other whispering behind his back that he was one of the ringleaders of the wildest gang of cutthroats the border had ever known. Turk had never heard of anyone saying such things to Bill's face.

He meandered the length of the gallery, wondering what had fetched Bill to a place like Silver Lake. He slapped at a persistent mosquito and water lapped the bottoms of the boats beyond the tamarisks. Roman 4 came into his thinking again and he tried to imagine what Bill would have done and a woman's laugh, coming off the lake, called up tantalizing visions of the taffy haired Holly. He growled. "You goddamn fool!" and went back inside.

The games were packed three deep in the card room and blue layers of smoke swirled and drifted under the green shades of the lamps. Clack of chips and clink of glasses. Talk curled around him like the voice of a thousand locusts.

No trouble here. He pushed on through and stepped into the bar as a burst of applause hammered the walls with its din. This was for the establishment's latest sensation, Rosarita, a Zincali dancer according to the billing; but Turk had overheard Arch telling Flack she was an alley cat the boss had picked up with a bottle of pulque in the *barrio libre*. Turk had watched her before. He stayed to see her again.

She was dark as a wood cutter. Golden eyes and black hair. A tawny panther of a girl in scarlet rags, sombrero and naked feet. Possibly a gypsy, Turk thought, but no Zincali. Her bones were too fine for an Indian; she had a different shape of face.

She'd been coming down the stairs. Now she paused to flash white teeth at the assemblage. She was insolence personified. The applause became deafening. She pulled off her hat and set it sailing over their heads. It was slanting toward Turk when a dozen hands flashed up, all hungrily reaching. Two pulled it down within three feet of his own outstretched arm. A man swore in angry protest. Turk saw a fist lash out, heard it strike against flesh. The red sombrero disappeared, was thrust aloft and shaken vigorously.

Curly Bill had it.

Turk pushed the sock back into his pocket. The girl made a face and Bill's laugh rang out and he called something to her that was lost in the uproarious cheering. "Rosarita! Come on, Sweetness, dance for us!"

You might have guessed she was the toast of Tucson the way that bunch of hombres yelled. She accepted the acclaim with scornful eyes and came onto the room's tiny stage as though it belonged to her, untwining the tattered scarf from her hair. The bull fiddle, the guitars and the five string banjo cut into the din with a quick beat of chords. The shouts died away. The roll of a drum began to build up excitement.

She jingled the coins on her wrists, tapped a foot. Suddenly the wild whipped-up music caught her, caught her up the way wind catches up dust and papers, spinning her across the boards of the stage in a pulse thumping blur of scarlet cloth and bare legs. She came out of it stamping her feet and head bobbing, the black mop of her hair flung straight up and then down to the clack of the castanets in her fingers. The music's weird rhythm was immeasurably quickened and she went spinning away like a leaf in a gale, skirt and jacket vibrating and twirling like a pair of red ropes against which her willowy body flashed naked.

It caught Turk's breath as it had before. It caught the rest of them, too. Applause struck the walls in solid crashes of sound. Gold and silver coins bounced and rolled about her feet while she refastened the jacket and eyed the crowd insolently thorugh the tumbled mass of her midnight hair.

She flung it back off her face completely ignoring them, down on her haunches gathering up the bright plunder.

Curly Bill started toward her through the crowd, the chinstrapped hat a blob of color where it dangled from his arm, shoving men off his brawny elbows uncaringly.

Then Turk saw something that turned his eyes sharply narrow. The man Bill had used his fist on was moving, gliding after him silent as a stalking cat. Sensing trouble Turk plunged after them.

Someone got in his way and by the time he'd ducked around Bill had reached the platform. He had one hand on it, bending forward, and the girl turned her face to peer up at him.

The second man, a Mexican dressed like a *charro*, was almost up to him. Turk saw the flash of steel and, ripping the sock from his pocket, plunged forward, striking blindly.

The blow missed the man's head and struck his hunched shoulder. The knife clattered from his hand. Then Turk was into him, slugging and taking his fists in return. The man's eyes flashed with hatred; he was wild to get loose. The blast of a gun ripped through the uproar, in those narrow confines the sound becoming enormous. The Mexican staggered back against a crush of other Mexicans, the frozen strain of their faces etched upon skin that was like pounded putty in the smoky flare of the lamps. The whites of the wounded man's eyes rolled up into his head and he half twisted, crumpling, spilling into Turk's legs.

Turk staggered back. There was a long-barreled pistol in Curly Bill's fist. The gray stench of powder-smoke swirled from its snout and the slitted stare back of it was like polished jet. The girl sprang erect, snatching her hat and whirling stairward. The room was a blur of shocked white faces. Turk put his hand against Bill's chest. "Quick man—move! Git up them stairs!"

Bill was going to argue. Turk gave him a shove. The planes of Bill's cheeks showed a dark rush of anger. He tipped up his gun. Its bore looked big as a cannon's.

"You want to git us *both* killed?"

Curly Bill snarled, furious. "You think I'd run from a greaser!"

A growl came out of the crowd. Someone shouted. Back of the bar Arch yelled: "Tie into him!"

Turk saw the flash of a bottle sail past their heads, saw it burst in a shower of glass on the stair rail. The second bouncer, Grigsby, shoved a popeyed face through the cardroom door. Turk saw his hand drive hipward. Flame roared in Turk's face and he thought for a second his eardrums were broken. Grigsby grabbed at his middle and folded into the wall.

"Get outa my way, Red!"

That was Arch again. His voice streaked like a gate hinge. Turk saw the sawed-off coming over the bar. Bill saw it too and leaped stairward. Turk almost stepped on his heels in his hurry.

Maybe Arch was afraid of hitting Turk; he didn't fire. Other men weren't so squeamish. Five slugs knocked holes in the plaster of the stairwell before Turk made the landing and scuttled upward out of sight.

He saw the dancer's bare feet flying down the hall. "Never mind the girl—" he panted. "Take the first unbarred door you git hold of!"

Bill did. It was China's. There was a man by the bed trying to get into his pants. Bill cracked him over the head with his gun barrel. The man toppled backwards. China cursed in several languages.

"Out of the window," Turk gasped. "We'll have to go down those posts."

Bill was halfway over the rail when Turk got through the window. Turk did not do any lingering either. Half the barroom was coming by the sound from the stairs. He swung over the rail and let go. He thought the ground must have driven his knees through his shoulders. He heard Bill running.

Bill swung back. "Which way's the stables?"

Turk got onto his feet. "No time for—that. Got to git through them trees." Bill was off like a shot. Turk, quartering after him, heard the bunch from the bar spilling out across the balcony. A cloud passed across the light from the moon. There were shouts from the balcony. A shotgun's racket filled the air with shrill whining. Something whipped at Turk's coat skirts; then he was diving into the tamarisks.

Curly Bill came out of the shadows. "There ain't nothin' out here—what I want is a horse!"

"Yeah," Turk panted. "Like to have one myself. Come on. There's some boats around here some-place."

Curly Bill stopped short. "Boats!" Turk saw his face twist around. "I ain't gittin' in no boat—"

"Then stay here," Turk growled, too worried to stop and argue. He was a little riled, too, consider-ing the changes he was taking. In the gloom of the windy shoreline he found three boats pulled up with their bottoms half out of the water. He grabbed the oars out of two and caught hold of the other one. "If you're comin' jump in."

"They'll pick us off like settin' ducks!"

Turk got his pistol out of his boot and tucked it inside the waistband of his black gambler's trousers. He put the extra oars in the boat. He was sliding the boat into the water when Bill, snarling under his breath, got it.

Turk could hear those fellows dropping off the balcony, could hear them shouting and cursing as they ran circling and panting through the roundabout shadows. Because of the trees and the clouds which covered the moon about all he could make out was the black slant of the tavern's roof, but at least a part of the racket seemed to be coming straight toward them. He jumped aboard with a final shove and caught up an oar.

Bill was still muttering. Turk glanced at the sky. In what looked to be seconds the moon would be free. He told Bill: "Git that white hat off and keep out of sight." He didn't wait to see if Bill minded; he put his knees on the leaky bottom and used an oar like a pole. When he couldn't touch bottom he used the oar for a paddle. They had more oars than he knew what to do with. He was scared to try rowing.

"I don't think they'll look for us out here," he whispered, staring up at the clouds again, "but if they spot us don't throw any lead at them. If they ever make sure who we are they'll git horses."

They made another thirty feet. "Here they come," Bill growled.

They were fifty yards off shore by then. The

bunch were beating the tamarisks and jabbering in Spanish. The boat drifted on for another ten feet and then a yell sailed up and the whole push came boiling out to the shoreline. Turk pulled in his oar and shouted, "What the hell ails you?" not reckoning they could see any better than he could.

They didn't fire anyway. They asked in Spanish if he'd seen two gringos in big hats. Turk replied in their lingo that he was trying to catch fish. He heard them do some more muttering. The moon came out and Turk sank back as the bunch on the shore cut off through the trees still arguing.

In the back of the boat Bill got up on a seat trying to squeeze some of the water out of his soaked pantlegs. "I'd as lief be shot as drowned!"

"You got a hat," Turk said. "Start bailin' if you're worried."

Bill took the remark seriously. He got to work on the water. He kept right on working until they reached the other side. Turk poled the boat into the reeds and got out, Bill following clumsily. Brush came down to within a few feet of the shore. When they got through it they emptied their boots out. "Road to town," Turk said, "will be over that way," pointing. "We might stay a lot more healthy if we keep plumb away from it."

Bill, snorting, struck off toward it, Turk reluctantly following.

Before long he wished his boots were several sizes larger. The wet leather bound on his ankles had made his feet burn. He moved quiet as he could and kept his ears peeled. Curly Bill said finally and rather testily Turk thought, "You hadn't no call to take chips in this deal—Why'd you do it?"

Turk shrugged.

"Women!" Bill said, and shook his head disgustedly. He didn't speak again till they came limping into town. After they'd gone half a block he said grudgingly, "Worked with cattle, ain't you?"

"I've chased a few," Turk nodded.

"What do they call you?"

"Turkey Red."

Bill pulled up, astonished. "Well, by Gawd!" he said, and chuckled. "You're the guy that kilt that squatter!"

He didn't say any more until Levin's hotel was in front of them, dark and silent except for a lamp's pallid gleam above the abandoned desk by the stairwell. He swung around then and faced Turk. "You ever git in a tight, boy, you call on Curly Bill."

Turk had figured to put up at Levin's himself but he couldn't very well after Bill had turned in there. Someway it didn't seem fitting. He didn't want Bill to think he was sucking around.

He clumped on down the street. There was a stage pulled up before the front of the Palace and he waited in the shadows until it rolled off, heading for Prescott. If Bill had heard about Fanshaw, Turk reckoned he was a marked man and he saw no use in taking needless chances. If the word got back to Wyatt Earp the marshal might decide to come over here.

He thought of finding a saloon. The streets were

deserted and, after tramping a few blocks, he swung back. To hell with Earp! Turk's feet were killing him. He saw the shine of lamps coming out of the stage depot. It was too late to get into a hotel now and, looking like he did, he didn't think a hotel would take him. He tugged his hat brim down and went into the depot's waiting room.

There was a drunk spraddled out on one of the benches. A couple of drummers swapping jokes were holding down another. The agent looked up from his desk behind the counter and put his face back into his papers when Turk limped past without speaking.

Turk dropped onto a bench. He wished the hell he dared take his boots off but was scared if he did he'd never get them back on. Tomorrow, he reckoned, he'd have to go out to the lake again, or send someone else, to pick up High Sailin. He sure didn't aim to get rooked out of his horse.

He took a squint at the clock. It had "Butterfield" wrote across it and showed later than he thought. He guessed maybe after he got High Sailin he would take a ride over around Skull Valley and get another ranch job if he could find a place needing help.

He went over the events of the evening. Curly Bill, by grab! Made a fellow feel pretty important. Kind of conspicuous, too. Wasn't many guys could boast helping out a gent of his caliber.

He shot a look at the drummers. They didn't even know he existed. Gave him a queer feeling, kind of. He reckoned their eyes would bug out if they was to know he had just been hobnobbing with Curly Bill Graham.

In this Arizona country Bill was by way of being about as talked about a jasper as Billy the Kid was over in New Mexico. All across these borders miles wild tales of Curly's daring furnished the exciting raw materials for supper yarning around the campfires of the cow camps. He was fast becoming a legend. Depending on where and to whom you listened you could hear pretty well nigh anything. He was champion of the small spreads. He was called a 'scourge' of the ranges. He was the Robin Hood of the wastelands. Snydicates and politics were doing their best to ruin the country, buying the courts and sheriffs. Everybody seemed to be out to *get* theirs. Curly Bill was the solitary rock in this time of transition; he stood foursquare for the cowboys. He didn't kowtow to anybody and the moguls walked in fear of his vengeance . . .

Turk must have drowsed. He was wakened by the racket of a just arrived stage. He could see people getting out of it, and one bunch of hostlers leading off the teams while another using plenty of "language" was hitching fresh broncs in their places.

The whip and guard came in with the mail pouch and the drummers got up and grabbed their bags and stomped out. There was enough damn noise for a herd of bull buffalos and plumb in the midst of it Turk's heart got to pounding like a battery of stamp mills.

He had to look twice before he could believe it, but there she was all right, dressed to kill and headed straight for him. Solomon in all his glory had never got up any carefuller to catch the eye.

She had a lavender cloth hat with feathers on

top of her gleaming high piled hair and a lavender dress with a smudge of black ribbon and lace around the collar, and a yellow cloth bag on a loop around her waist. A yellow parasol edged with lavender was clutched in her hand and there was four million pleats in the skirt she held up to keep from falling over it. Every guy in the place turned his face around to gawk and she sailed past them all, coming straight up to Turk.

His ears got hot and in a way he kind of wished that he was back at Silver Lake but, like most of his wishing, it didn't go him any good. She came up with her hand out—the one with the bag on it—and her face all lit up with surprise and excitement. "Turkey!" she exclaimed in that deep throaty voice that always chased tingles up and down his back gone. "But this is marvelous of you —I didn't expect you to *meet* me."

Turk muttered something, gulping, but might as well have saved his breath. She had hold of his arm now, smiling, looking up at him til you'd have thought they were honeymooners—leastways, he made no doubt everyone else had latched onto that notion.

"Well!" she said, pouting. "Aren't you even going to kiss me?"

Turk glared around at the grinning watchers. Holly, following his look, made a face and said, "Silly!" Then reached up a gloved hand and patted his cheek.

Turk guessed his mug looked like a fire had been built under it. He got hold of her elbow and started hustling her toward the door, making out not to hear or see a thing till they got through it.

"Where's your case?" he grunted, eyeing the heap of luggage the driver had set down beside the stage's back wheel.

"Right there—that one," she smiled, pointing.

He reached down and got a hand on it. She stood back, trim and neat as a basket of chips, and he could feel the old adam start to push and pummel and pound again. He had figured to be plumb done with her but, watching that tongue crawl across her red lips, was willing to admit he might have made a snap judgment.

She gave him one of her twisted smiles. "Where are you staying, Turk?"

He mighty near dropped her case on his foot. A dozen crazy notions got to larruping through his head, but the shining one that got him was that actually he *had* misjudged her. Either that or she'd changed her mind, and he was in no condition to find fault with miracles. It never occured to him to wonder how she had known he would be in Tucson.

He had trouble with his breathing.

Her eyes got big and sparkly. She slipped a hand through his arm and hugged the arm against her. "They'd remember me at the Levin—couldn't you find us something out on the side streets? It doesn't really matter except that we're together, does it?"

It surely didn't to Turk. He couldn't get his thoughts untangled or the scent of her out of his thinking long enough to give any real thought to it. He hoped this meant she'd decided to team with him permanent; it didn't seem like the moment to jaw about it though and any suspicions he may have had he choked down as being unworthy, wanting desperately to believe her sweet surrender was complete.

With her squeezing his arm against her like that he couldn't hardly tell up from down. Any place would do for the balance of the night—it was pretty near light already, he thought anxiously, wondering if they could find a place now. In the morning—later, he reckoned, they had better hit out for the border; Ruebusch wasn't likely to take this lying down. Turk could speak enough Mex to get by. He would get him a job with some big hacendado. When they'd got enough dough he'd get some stock of his own . . .

He found them a room at a place on South Meyer.

It wasn't right, he knew that; knew that nothing was like to ever make it right either, but few things in this world were the way a man would want them.

He had most of the answers. Still it wasn't like he had figured it would be. Time they got to the room most of his lift had worn off and his thoughts weren't tracking the way he would have had them. A queer unease had gotten into him and it made him irascible and clumsy. She was willing all right; she was at him no sooner than he had got the door fastened.

"Plenty of time for that," he said scowling. "What about Fanshaw? What did Ruebusch do?"

She gave him a kind of odd look and tossed her hair back. "He rode into Tombstone and told Fred

White you'd had a quarrel with Fanshaw and killed him."

White was town marshal, not a Deputy U.S. Marshal like Earp was.

"Why White?" Turk asked.

"He told Johnny Behan too." Behan was a deputy sheriff. "Said you were always getting into fights with people, that he'd finally had to fire you. White said it was *uncommon funny* that right after you'd shot him Fanshaw's dam got broke open so conveniently. Ruebusch said the old man blew up the dam himself after they'd settled their differences with five thousand dollars. He said he imagined you and Fanshaw had been in cahoots and that you'd probably killed him in an agrument over the money."

Turk scowled in silent fury but when Holly came snuggling up again he took hold of her like he meant it. Her eyes went shut. He could feel her tremble. Her hands came up and pulled down his head. He felt her mouth spread and it was just like kicking the roof off the world.

They were both breathing hard when she let go of him. She reached for her fastenings. "Tomorrow," Turk said, "we'll light a shuck for the border . . ."

Her eyes looked like two pieces of glass. "Have we got to go through all that again?"

"Through all what?"

"That stuff about me going off with you."

Turk said tight and careful, "What about it?"

"I'm not going, that's what about it. Tomorrow or any other time."

50

Turk was staring but he wasn't really seeing her. He got back into his coat and picked up his hat.

Her lips curled. "Always running!" She pushed back her hair. "Where are you off to now?"

"I'm goin' to join Curly Bill."

She looked at his set face and laughed. Then the jeer fell out of her eyes. "You crazy damn fool—"

Turk pulled the door shut behind him.

# FOUR

THIS WAS ARIZONA in the time of the locusts, a hair-triggered realm in the throes of transition. A great unrest was setting in all across the American nation. The East was paving the way for the spectacular rise of Boss Tweed and a motley host of imitators and, across the line in New Mexico, the great trading monopoly of Murphy-Dolan had its back to the wall in that fight for survival which historians have recorded as the Lincoln County War; Billy the Kid was running wild and thumbing his nose at Lew Wallace; and that great cattle thief, John Chisum, was nearing the end of his string.

The country's morals had done a flipflop and all over the vast and sparsely settled Southwest armed banditry was paying enormous dividends. Tombstone was in its heyday and honkytonk row set the pace men lived and all too frequently died by. It was the day of the cattle kings, of great combines. Ruthlessness was rampant. Millions of longhorned cattle roved the great ranges of Chihuahua and Sonora and many a respectable American was engaged in hazing this beef across the line—so many, in fact, that it had become an established business. And there was no one more expert at promoting this industry than rollicking, burly Curly Bill Graham.

He was rightly dubbed the "scourge of the ranges." He frequently shanghaied a thousand head at one swoop and was not averse to selling gringo cattle to the dons. The Mexican steers he disposed of to contractors supplying the San Carlos and other Indian agencies. He sold them to frontier slaughterhouses and to unscrupulous ranchers who shipped them East to Cincinnati, Kansas City, Chicago and St. Louis. New cattlemen bought from him to augment their herds which he frequently depleted for his sales below the line. He was well on his way to becoming the "international menace" and had already been the subject of several debates in Congress.

It was a mark of the times and a commentary on law enforcement that he went freely about his nefarious business at will. He was a familiar and jovial customer in the gambling houses and saloons of booming Tombstone. A reputation for wildness, even for downright banditry in other places, was openly winked at by denizens of this silver camp; they were much too busy acquiring wealth of their own to be overly concerned with the didos of the cow crowd.

Sometimes Bill rode with forty men at his back; he was seldom to be seen without a half dozen and was no guy to yell boo at. For all his robust good looks, his uproarious pranks and dimples he was always, grimly under these, strictly a man with his eye on the main chance. And deadly as a timber wolf. Practically every outlaw in the southeastern end of the Territory owed some form of allegiance to him; he was tied in also with the vested interests, the political setup which was making Arizona such a paradise for wanted men. Johnny Behan, the Tucson sheriff's deputy for the Tombstone end of Pima County, was openly friendly as were many of the country's ranchers. It was not too greatly to be wondered at that a youngster of Turkey Red's antecedents and naive impressionability, seeing only this fellow's outward self and the general esteem and standing accorded him, should seek to make himself over in Bill's image.

Turk lost no time in making for Curly Bill's stamping grounds. There was a strong streak of rashness woven through his nature which, given focus by his need of belonging and fired by rankling memories of Holly's scornful refusal to take him seriously, sent him across the wasteland miles with no care or thought for the consequences. He would show her, by God—he would show them all! A full moon looked down from the blue-black skies as he reined High Sailin up out of the mesquite brush and greasewood of the desert and followed the stage road on to the mesa to see the lamps of the silver camp gleaming like drops of soapy water through the night.

Away from the town the darkness didn't look so black. Off to the north by a little east the Dragoon Mountains raised silvered escarpments looking lost and lonesome in that immense spread of distance which beyond was called Sulphur Springs Valley. Northwest the humpbacked shoulders of the Rincons thrust up out of the San Pedro gloom. West, and much closer, were the peaks of the Whetstones looking like steeples whacked out of black paper. Farther, south-west, the lines of the Hauchucas made dim blue tracery, and dead south stood the Mules between this mesa and the border, a scant thirty miles by horseback. Due east were the Cherrycows, brooding like a sleepy hen above the San Bernardino and the pale Pedregosas.

A wind was rolling up off the flatlands, not truly cold but strongly hinting of cold weather to come, puffing and snorting like a bronc with the wheezes. Turk pulled his gambler's coat a bit more snugly about his shoulders and turned up the scanty collar to protect a throat not yet used to being without its neck rag.

He stared morosely at the lights of Tombstone, not so easy now that he was here about his actual chances of hooking on with Graham. A lobo wolf's howl coming off some ridgetop uncomfortably reminded him of Deputy Marshal Wyatt Earp who was so rapidly building a rep in this town. But the place was teeming, everyone said so, and among the six thousand people headquartering in the town he guessed, with reasonable caution, he shouldn't have too much trouble keeping out of Earp's sight. Fred White wouldn't know him or Earp either, probably. Earp and his brothers had plenty to do keeping peace in the place and he was over here primarily to collect back taxes which should be a big enough chore to keep any agent occupied.

Turk cuffed his flat topped felt a little lower

over his eyes and dug High Sailin a poke in the ribs to let him know he still had a man aboard of him. Maybe Bill wouldn't choose to remember their meeting. But he was said to be a man which kept his word no matter what; and after all, by grab, Turk *had* done him a favor.

He wondered again what it would really be like to be riding in the company of Curly Bill. A pretty breathtaking business, he reckoned. He was a pretty fair hand with cattle; maybe Bill would use him on some of his forays below the line . . .

His unease grew almost to the proportions of premonition while he strove unsuccessfully to convince himself that Earp would not deem him worth bothering about. Hadn't Frank Leslie—him they called "Buckskin" on account of his preference for that sort of clothing—dropped Mike Killeen in a gun fight right on the steps of the Commerical Hotel? Hadn't another guy called "King" shot and killed young Johnnie Wilson in the very middle of Allen Street with people thicker than flies all around him? And both of them turned loose! Both of them tough eggs that cared no more about upping the death rate than they would about weevils getting baked in their biscuits. Still and all Turk couldn't feel comfortable. Wyatt Earp was a very persevering kind of man, and he was friendly with Ruebusch. Which might make all the difference.

Just in these few weeks he had been gone Turk noticed the signs of change and growth. The town had spread all over hell's kitchen. And racket—Cripes! He shook his head in astonished wonder.

Fabulous fortunes were associated with Tombstone and fabulous violence in the eyes of the East. The town was being featured in the big eastern dailies. Boston, New York and Philadelphia papers had their own correspondents living right on the ground. Gamblers—"high rollers"—were considered the equal of anyone. Harlots and purse snatchers tramped cheek by jowl along the streets with respectable citizens and sometimes, he thought, you couldn't tell them apart. He had heard that White favored restricting the women to particular sides of certain designated streets. He was honest, Turk reckoned, as the country would let him be, though some folks figured he listened too much to Earp.

These Tombstone people were great ones for bragging. They took a heap of pride in their iniquities and boisterousness and, according to their tell, things held smart in New York and San Francisco were hauled by the freighters or by relays of fast riders to be admired or served up with gusto in the tonier establishments of this roaring camp. You could get the best coffin varnish, the finest squabs and oysters, the flossiest women—almost anything imaginable, so long as you had the price or the connections.

It was the most celebrated town in the Territory. One mile high and a place where the roofs could be took off for anything.

The wind didn't seem to be blowing near as gusty by the time Turk got to where the sounds of the place enveloped him. Where the stage road became the main street, which was called Allen, a crew of carpenters working in the light of flaring lanterns were rushing a new clapboarded building to completion. Wagons of all kinds and descriptions appeared to be everywhere and cursing mule skinners and ranch hands, and even a sprinkling of horse soldiers in blue coats and yellow neckerchiefs, were shouting, swearing, howling and laughing till the din was like nothing Turk had ever heard in his life.

On his left as he'd entered town he'd seen the clutter of shacks and mud boxes of the Mexican quarter. The Chinese quarter came next, north on Second and back off a piece to the right. Traffic got heavier and he found it harder to wedge High Sailin through. By the time he reached the Can Can, a hash house at the northwest corner of Allen and Fourth just beyond the stage barns and O.K. Corral, the signs of growth were everywhere apparent. And deadfalls. Violins, banjos, guitars and tinpanny pianos were whooping things up to a fine noisy frenzy and there was plenty of light along both sides of the way. Plenty of people too— the board walks were jammed with them, talking their jaws off and tramping every whichway.

He put the big gelding across Fourth and passed the Occidental Hotel on the right, the Cosmopolitan on the left with the Occidental Saloon alongside of it and, over again on his right, the blazing-windowed front of the Grand Hotel. The snarl of traffic was getting so bad his progress was almost at a standstill when Turk squeezed High Sailin over against a line of racked horses and stopped, blinded and half strangled in a lemon fog of dust whipped up by the rumbling passage of a train of heavy ore wagons.

He was wedged there for ten minutes before he found a chance to get moving again, and then only at a snail's pace. A boisterous bunch of what looked like cowpunchers pushed through the green batwings of Bob Hatch's saloon which was next to the Alhambra; and a couple of doors along he saw the Crystal Palace's sign.

They had a little more room after they got across Fifth. Sixth, as Turk knew, was where most of the cribs were, the hangouts of Rowdy Kate and Dutch Annie, Blonde Mary and Crazy Horse Lil, Madame Moustache and a whole flock of others. He was able to wedge High Sailin up to a tie rail before he got quite as far as Sixth, about seven doors beyond the Arcade Saloon and on Allen's south side just ahead of some empty lots.

Waiting for a break in the traffic he crossed to get onto Allen's north walk, thinking he might find Bill in the Arcade. It didn't seem to him very likely that in any such seething crush of humanity he was going to be recognized as the fellow being hunted for the killing of Fanshaw. Two-thirds of these people had probably never heard of Fanshaw.

Some of Turk's caution, along with his uneasiness, began to wear off. When he reached the Arcade Saloon he pushed into it. The bar was packed six deep already and as soon as he was able to get turned around he headed for the street, letting the walk's crowd jostle him back down along to Fifth.

Where in the world, he wondered, did all these folks put up at?

The buildings were mostly of frame and adobe,

a few of them actually having second floors instead of the foolish false fronts so much in vogue throughout the West's cowtowns. Wooden awnings projected out over the board walks which flanked the front of each establishment, and the walks were flanked by horse crammed hitch rails along both sides of Allen's sixty-foot width.

As he came to where Fifth made its slash square across it a string of wagons groaning beneath high piles of lumber fresh cut and hauled from the Cherrycows appeared; a careening stage jolted in from the left and the dust got so thick you could taste it. All around Turk folks were swearing and shouting, declaring wagons ought to be kept off of Allen.

When he was able to clear his streaming eyes the crowd he'd got locked into was half across the intersection. A bunch of skallyhootin' horse-backers came out of the wagons' fog, tearing into Fifth and sending everyone jumping to keep from being run down. Turk swore at them with the rest and barreled on into the lights of the Crystal Palace. He couldn't have got into that place if he had wanted to.

He gave up the hunt, thinking maybe tomorrow he would have better luck. Of course Bill might not even be around, might be off on one of his cattle gathering trips or holed up with some woman—he was quite a hand with the ladies by repute.

Bob Hatch's bar wasn't quite so crowded and Turk was able to get in although not to wet his whistle. He pushed on through to the rear and shoved open the door into Bob's back room. There was a game going on, draw poker by the looks, and Curly Bill was in it with the dollars stacked high in front of him. One stack was gold—double eagles.

Turk closed the door and stood back against the wall, uneasy again now he'd run Bill to earth. After sweating the game for about twenty minutes Turk saw one of the players pitch down his cards in disgust. "I'm strapped!" he growled, and got up and went out, viciously slamming the door shut behind him. A couple of the players laughed. They spread out a little and went on with the deal. Somebody opened, a couple of gents raised and Bill raised them; the two others dropped out. The opener took one. Both the raisers took three. Bill stood pat. The opener showed a pair of jacks and got out. The first raiser bet fifty dollars, the second man hiking it another thirty. Bill saw these and kicked in another hundred. Both men quit and Bill raked in the chips with a laugh. "Pair of sixes," he said, but nobody asked to see them.

"About time we were breakin' this up," someone said and Bill, lifting his stare, saw Turk. "Well, look what's here," he said, and all their heads turned. "That's the kid Wyatt Earp's been huntin' for—feller that downed Fanshaw."

Turk could feel the riled blood burning into his cheeks and he knew deep inside him with a cold desperate sinking that he'd been a fool to come here, and a bigger fool to have taken Bill's gratitude for granted. Probably Bill didn't even figure that Turk had helped him getting away from that bunch at Silver Lake that night. The words strung. Gratitude or not, Bill hadn't needed to tell the rest of these yaps that Wyatt Earp was after him!

With the blood still roaring through him Turk saw Bill wave a careless hand, heard him say in that same half hoorahing tone, "Don't let them duds or that starved look throw you—feller's apt to gaunt up some ridin' fer Ruebusch. Boys, meet Turkey Red."

Several of them nodded, a shade more interest in their stares; and Turk, with temper cooling, understood Bill had been trying to help him, trying to make him appear more acceptable to those tough hands around the table. "With the right kind of chance," Bill said, "I figure he'll pull his weight with our bunch." He grinned at Turk. "Guy behind all them whiskers is Jim Hughes," he said. "Next gent's Tom McLowery—big rancher over towards Animas. That rusty-haired hellion is known as Tex Willbrandt. Squatty one's Jake Gauze."

Only Tom McLowery bothered to stick his hand out. He had a lean capable looking face and a quick strong grip that impressed Turk favorably. Gauze looked distinctly hostile. The other pair just looked at him without any feeling one way or the other.

Bill said, "We got a little business to git off our chests. Tex, you and Turk sift along to Frank Stilwell's; we'll pick you up there soon's we git away. Where'd you leave your horse, Turk?"

"Over by them empty lots across from the Arcade."

"All right. You boys shove along then."

Tex ducked his head and Turk followed him out. As they pushed along through the thinning crowds that were still afoot on the walk outside Turk covertly eyed Tex Willbrandt more carefully. He had quite a reputation as a rough and tumble fighter and was no slouch with a six-shooter. Lath thin he was, a steel spring kind of man with a reputed penchant for peppermint lozenges, of which he had several in his mouth at the moment judging by the whiff Turk had caught of his breath. His clothes sagged loosely from the bony shoulders. He had a rust colored mustache, streaked and wild above his mouth, and roan bristles sprouting thickly from the jut of his short broad chin. A faded blue wipe was knotted loosely about his neck and alkali grit was ground into the whole look of him.

Halfway down the block he said something Turk didn't catch, there was so much gab around him. Willbrandt leaned closer. "I said you sure you know what you're doin'?"

Turk looked at him blankly.

"Gettin' mixed up with Curly Bill," Willbrandt said. "Hardcase outfit. No place for a feller with his whole life ahead of him."

Turk's ears got hot and resentment welled up in him. Willbrandt's pale Texas eyes read the signs and he said dryly, "Understand, it's no skin off my nose what you do. But now's the time to get goin' if you aim to pull out."

Turk said thickly: "I know what I'm doin'. When I need a wet nurse—"

"Don't call on me," Willbrandt said. He nodded darkly. "I left my bronc back of the feed store. I'll meet you where you left yours." He didn't wait for an answer but ducked away through the crowd.

Turk, scowling after him a moment, moved on. It wasn't easy to put into words the things he felt about Bill; he was all the things Turk wanted to be but knew, deep inside him, he likely never would. He didn't have the size of assurance. He didn't have the ready grin, the jovial laugh or the reputation—though that last, he reckoned darkly, was something he sure could latch onto. And traveling in Bill's wake would be the quickest way to get started. Bill wasn't only big in himself; the way he did things was big, attention catching, important. Bill might be a thief but he was no two-bit thief.

And then, abruptly, the whole bottom dropped out of Turk's world. He stopped, frozen motionless, incapable even of swallowing.

Less than six strides away and coming straight for him was old I Personally Ruebusch, flanked by Strehl and Linderstrom. Strehl grinned nastily. Linderstrom kept his thoughts to himself.

All three of them pulled up about an arm's reach away with Strehl's fist dropping against the butt of his gun.

# FIVE

ALL ABOUT THEM people had stopped and now were frantically striving to get themselves out of the way. Ruebusch looked wild enough to burst his surcingle, too nearly berserk for that business of Fanshaw wholly to account for it; and Turk's mind leaped to Holly.

He licked dry lips.

In spite of everything though, the Roman 4 boss was making a rolling-eyed effort to hang onto his passions. "You were warned to stay out of this country," he said harshly, and then his fury got away with him. Thrusting his jaw within a half a foot of Turk's he snarled, "You sawed-off little whey-faced whelp! What have you done with my—"

Turk, pushed beyond caution, slammed a knee in his crotch and, when the man doubled over, hit him so hard he went back into Lindstrom all spraddled out and before Strehl could get his gun clear of leather Turk had his own dug into Strehl's belly.

Turk's face had gone white as a wagon sheet.

Strehl was scared, too. He understood that one grunt could put him under a box lid. "Go on and draw," Turk rasped, "you white-livered polecat!"

Strehl's eyes looked ready to pop from their sockets and Linderstrom's jaws were clamped together so hard gray ridges of muscle stood out from them like ropes.

Ruebusch was still gagging and there was no telling what might have been the outcome of it if Johnny Behan and a couple of his sidekicks had not come running up just then. All the rest of the crowd that wasn't wedged into doorways had ducked plumb into the jammed traffic of the street; but Behan had hopes of being sheriff come next election and likely figured this a chance for catching a few votes from Roman 4.

"What's the matter here—what's goin' on?" he called, shoving up.

Strehl knew better than to open his mouth and Ruebusch, still moaning, hadn't yet caught up with his breath. Turk said, "This hogleg is set on a hair trigger. It's like to splatter this skunk hell west and crooked if you make any move to put your nose into it."

The under sheriff's eyes raked a fruitless look about him and apparently decided he'd got into the wrong stall. He backed down with a parched grin and took off, his companions following.

Turk, cooler now, pushed Strehl off his gun and moved far enough back to catch all three within its focus. "All right, you sinkers," he said gruffly, "git goin'."

It did his soul good to see the blotched look of

Linderstrom's mug. Ruebusch got himself up off the walk's dusty boards with his face like green cheese and pawed around for his dentures, but mostly Turk watched Linderstrom. "If this looks to you like a good night for dyin' don't let me stand in the way of your doin' it."

Ruebusch lurched off with Strehl right on his heels. Turk could hear the hard grating of Linderstrom's teeth but the man wheeled away without opening his mouth.

Turk's knees got so weak he nearly had to sit down.

He dropped the pistol back in his pocket and tried to pull himself together. That was coming too almighty close for comfort. He looked around for Willbrandt but didn't see anything of him. Traffic was starting to pull out of its tangle and people were fanning out onto the walk again when it crossed his mind Ruebrusch might go to Earp. He'd heard someone saying earlier Earp had recently resigned his tax job with the sheriff to support Bob Paul in the coming elections, but he was still deputy marshal and probably still friends with the Roman 4. It looked a mighty good time for Turk to make himself scarce.

He cast a glance over his shoulder and saw Bill and some other gents coming out of Hatch's Saloon. Watching his chance, Turk cut across the street and made a bee line for the hitchrail where his horse was. He hadn't covered half the distance when a man cut in ahead of him bound in the same direction.

The light was poorer over here because the

fronts of a lot of these buildings were dark, but something in the way that yonder man moved narrowed Turk's stare. He could feel his muscles begin to pull tight. The man's head swung around and Turk went flat against a store front.

The man was Fred White, the Tombstone town marshal!

Turk scarcely dared breathe.

He didn't know what to do. He didn't imagine White had spotted him but if the lawman wasn't on the prowl for him what was he doing over here and heading so pat in the direction of Turk's horse?

Turk wished he had never come back to this country. He felt a powerful urge to grab the nearest racked bronc and tear out of this. But an unwillingness to abandon High Sailin stopped him. He reckoned a man was a plain damn fool to let himself get so worked up about a horse.

White had moved on again. Turk moved too, sticking close to the buildings. The star packer was stepping out faster now, striding past High Sailin like he wasn't even there.

Turk shook his head. That White was a sharp one. He watched him cut into the vacant lots and vanish, fading into the shadows.

He was cute, all right. On account of the buildings cutting off Turk's view he couldn't make out if White had stopped or not, or which way he'd been headed. He might even have swung back, be waiting right now behind that last building.

Turk was mad and scared but not yet plumb

foolish. He wasn't anxious to get his neck stretched—not even for High Sailin. But he didn't want to give the brown up unless he had to. He cautiously edged nearer to the corner of that last building, belatedly aware of a deal of cater-wauling back of him.

Curly Bill's bunch, he saw, twisting his head. Noisier than hell emigrating on cart wheels. He noticed that a couple of them were flourishing pistols. Shouting and shooting and howling like Apaches, they came tromping along through the heavy dust, singing and bellering and calling ribald remarks. They weren't using the north walk and no one else was either, not with them throwing all that lead so promiscuous. Glass was breaking all over and Turk could hear Bill's hearty guffaws riding high above everything. There wasn't any real harm in it. Clowning, that's all it was.

The vacant lots were just ahead of Turk. This last building had a narrow railed porch tacked onto the front of it and was set back a stride or two to accommodate this appendage — a rooming house by the look of it. Yes, there was a sign on the door. Turk's glance swiveled streetward. High Sailin with pricked ears was watching the yonder commotion and blowing softly through his nose like he couldn't make up his mind if he should snort or send out a challenge.

Turk was about two jumps from the hitchrack when he caught the slam of a door. Seemed to have come from the shadows of the empty lots and now, away back, he saw the bulk of a shack and a man running from it, coming this way and coming fast —Fred White! Three other shapes back of him were cutting west around the rooming house to hit the street behind Turk.

There was no time for thinking. He could dive for High Sailin and give White a target or he could try to get back down the street.

He did neither. He fastened a hand on the railing of the rooming house porch and pulled himself over, desperately hoping in this gloom they wouldn't see him.

He hadn't hardly got settled before White reached the street. He ran right out into it. Curly Bill's racket stopped. Turk glimpsed the men who'd been with Bill taking off like scared rabbits. He saw Bill swing a look around and then, still brandishing his pistol, break into a run toward the lots.

White cut him off. "Give mc that gun!" he said.

"I wasn't doin' none o' that shootin'—"

"You give me that gun!" White cried, furious.

The two weren't a dozen steps away from Turk's concealment. Bill, grumbling, held out the pistol, butt forward. That much Turk saw plain. And White reaching for it. Then something blurred at the corners of his eyes and he saw the other three —the ones who had left White to swing around the building—flit past the end of the porch, sprinting streetward.

"Watch out!" Turk yelled, never stopping to think.

Everything happened at once then. With the yell still pouring out of him Turk saw Wyatt Earp throw his arms around Bill. He couldn't understand how White had got hold of Bill's gun barrel but he saw flame gout out of it. White, screaming, doubled over, both hands clutched to the front of him. Bill's hat fell off and Earp bent his own gun over the top of Bill's head and Bill went down sprawling.

Turk saw Earp drop beside them, squatting on his boot heels. Muzzle lights bloomed and Turk guessed that was Bill's crowd firing out of the dark, trying to cut Earp down. He could see the dust jumping up all around Earp. The two men who had dashed out there with Earp crouched nearby firing back at them. Turk heard Earp shout through the uproar. "Put that fire in Fred's coat out," and saw the nearest man—it looked like one of Earp's brothers—squirming forward and bend over him, slapping.

The racket of guns dimmed away and quit. Morgan Earp, looking up, said, "He ain't goin' to make it."

Wyatt Earp got to his feet. "Take him over to the shack. Keep your gun on Bill, Virg. I'll get them others."

"One done the hollerin' was on that porch," Morgan threw after him.

And that jarred Turk into some awareness of his own fix. His stomach muscles knotted and chills clawed his back as he watched Earp wheel toward him with that long-barreled six-shooter tipped up in front of his chest.

No one had to tell Turk about the prowess of that gent. Wyatt Earp was hell on wheels. The toughest tin-badge on the border.

Sweat cracked through the pores of Turk's hide. If he fought he'd be cut down in his tracks and if he gave himself up he'd swing for Fanshaw's killing, damned by the talk right out of his own mouth!

# SIX

"PSST—IN HERE!"

Turk guessed he must have died a thousand deaths before he caught that guarded whisper. There wasn't anything wrong with his legs though. He was through the crack of that roominghouse door before the oncoming marshal had taken three steps. He got a faint whiff of fragrance and guessed it was a girl who was easing the door shut. The tiny clink of the bolt sounded monstrously loud.

He couldn't see a thing but felt her hand touch his arm. He felt her breath against his cheek. "Pull off your boots."

With a sense of shock he knew her then—the Zincali dancer from Silver Lake. A dozen questions pummeled his mind while he got out of his boots and then her hand was in his, gently tugging him forward. "Stairs," she whispered, and he crept up them after her, holding close to the wall to keep the treads from creaking. He stumbled on the landing and half fell into her, feeling the willowly slenderness, smelling the clean sweet fragrance of her hair. They must have turned down a hall; she pulled him into a room, softly closing the door. Turk found a chair and jammed it under the knob.

The darkness was less opaque here, partially dispersed by reflected light from the street. He could see her standing near him, as intently listening as he was. He crossed to the window and, raising it a crack, put an ear to it. He didn't hear anything but ordinary street sounds. He didn't relax either. He wheeled toward her again, remembering her golden eyes and black hair, knowing he couldn't stay here, his mind still whirling with the clamor of questions prodded up by that business of Bill and Fred White and Wyatt Earp and his brothers. He was worried about Bill and about himself too, and knowing Earp's rep as he did he had a right to be.

"I don't think," she said, "we'd better chance a light."

Turk stared through the shadows. He said, "I've got to get out."

"I know. They're bound to search. Would it help if I took your horse around back?"

Turk said, "It sure would. I think a heap of that horse." He thought of something else, the danger she might run in helping the escape of a man who had Wyatt Earp on his trail; and he shook his head at her. "No," he said gruffly, "you've risked plenty as it is."

She must have sensed his confusion. She came nearer, saying softly, "I'd be glad to get him for you."

He took a turn about the room, made vaguely

uneasy by her tone. He swung back. "If you're really bustin' to do somethin'," he said, "you might take care of him for me till I can send somebody after him."

"I think you can trust me. There are box elder trees just outside the back door. You could wait here while I ride your horse around."

Turk wanted the horse and she made it sound easy. "All right," he said finally, "if—"

"You'd better count on giving me five or ten minutes. As soon as the way is clear I'll bring him in from behind. Do you know where you'll be going?"

Turk, about to blurt Charleston, said instead, "I'll find a place. How'd you know I was out there?"

"I'd better get your horse. We can talk about that later."

After she had gone he sank down in the chair she'd taken away from the door and pulled on his boots, removing his spurs and thrusting them into a pocket. But almost at once he was buckling them on again. If he needed them at all the need would be urgent and he'd better chance their racket than be caught with bare heels if he got into a jackpot.

He hoped Curly wasn't bad hurt. He was still disturbed over that business of the pistol. He felt positive he had seen Bill hold it out butt forward. How then had Fred White come to have hold of its barrel? It didn't make sense and yet how else, if White hadn't, could that bullet have crashed into him?

Turk got up and prowled the room, more bothered than he was admitting. And it wasn't just

75

White or his own fix—that girl bothered him too. She had saved his life. No getting around that part —but how had she known he was out there? Or in this town? And what was *she* doing here? He had an uncomfortable feeling she might have followed him, and that didn't make any sense to him either. Up till tonight he hadn't spoken ten words to her.

And there was the startled surprise he'd felt hearing her talk just now. At Silver Lake she'd spoken a kind of back alley English, regular foreigner lingo. And she was no Zincali—he'd have bet his boots on that!

He went to the door, quietly pulling it open. He listened a moment, hearing nothing to alarm him, and carefully felt his way to the pitch black head of the stairs. He was about to start down them when the creak of a board came up out of the darkness.

Turk's knees started shaking. His eyes stared wildly through the gloom, picturing it filled with gun-drawn possemen. But when after several moments nothing further had broken the quiet he attempted to convince himself it had been a timber settling.

He drew a long breath, feeling a fool to be getting so goosy over nothing. Bill wouldn't be standing here shaking like a ninny; he wouldn't be letting Turk trail with him if he thought Turk hadn't no more guts than this.

The thudding pound of Turk's heart slacked off a little. He wiped his hands on his pants and again took hold of the banister; and that was when he heard the stealthy whisper of moving feet. Frozen motionless he heard the feet pace the lower hall

76

and then the sound of a bolt carefully drawn from its socket. A low mutter of voices came up to him then and he waited no longer.

Back in the girl's room he went at once to the window, easing it up and raking the street with bitter eyes. He didn't see anyone watching. He didn't see any way of getting down from here either.

He pulled sheets off the bed and grabbed the blanket off the foot of it. They'd search the ground floor first. He left the girl's room, thinking there was bound to be a window at the hall's far end.

There was. He saw the dim square of it just as a thunderous knock shook a door down below. "Open up!" Earp's voice came to him, and then a jabber of protests under cover of which Turk got to the window. He pushed up the sash and saw the empty lots below him darkly shadowed by this building and the bulking shapes of a pair of tamarisk trees. He swiftly knotted together the untorn sheets and the blanket, only then discovering there was nothing to tie the top end to. Booted feet pulled groans from the treads of the stairway.

Turk stared desperately at the ground twelve feet below him, but there was nothing else for it. Letting go of the sheets he threw a leg over the sill, squirmed around and pulled his other leg out. He let himself down to the length of his arms, then let go of the sill and dropped.

Twelve feet was no great height and hanging by his fingers he didn't drop that far, but he dropped far enough to hit off balance and be thrown. And when he scrambled up his left ankle drove pain through him. He had to grit his teeth to put weight on it but he dared not stay where he was and he didn't dare go round to the back now, either—Earp would be sure to have somebody watching the back. Probably the front, too, but at least out front they'd not be watching so careful.

He limped into the deep shadows of the tamarisks, coming out on the side of them away from the building. Then he moved toward the street wanting to whistle but unable even to achieve that dubious cover. His throat was like cotton, his heart pounding madly.

He didn't see anyone in front of the rooming house, didn't see High Sailin either. But there were three horses tied at a rack across the street and he crossed diagonally toward these, ignoring those racked closer at hand. They'd be looking for him to grab the nearest horse he could get his legs around.

Pain from his hurt ankle pushed a cold sweat through the pores of his skin and he could see obliquely ahead of him the corner where Charlie Storms last year had gasped out his life with an unfired pistol still in his hand. The light was dimmer out here in the street than it had been when he'd got trapped on that porch but it still lacked a lot of being as poor as he could have wished for.

He had almost reached the north walk, with hope at last beginning to swell through him, when he saw a man with a rifle watching from the corner of a building two doors this side of the Arcade's entrance. Then he saw the other one. This second man was stepping into the street on an angle that would put him between Turk and the horses.

The shock of it almost choked off Turk's breathing. His face turned stiff and his legs were like lead and it was all he could do to keep his hand from his holster. But the man wasn't sure or he'd have brought up the rifle; he had both hands on it holding it squared across his thighs, chin a little forward as he waited for Turk to come up to him.

By a tremendous effort of will Turk kept to his course, fighting down the pull of his outraged nerves that would turn him aside, spook him into a run. He wouldn't get ten feet that way and he knew it; but it was hard—bitter hard, to limp up to that fellow, knowing what would happen if he got stopped now.

He was three feet away when the man with the rifle swung it around in grim focus. "Just a minute."

In the frozen calm of desperation everything else fell away from Turk but the black still shape of that man against lamplight. The man was not to be fooled with. It showed in the tone with which he said, "Where you off to?"

"Pick up my horse."

Although he could not make out the man's face against those lights Turk could feel the man's stare raking over him suspiciously.

"What's happened to your gun?"

Turk checked the impulse to look down at his holster. It took more will to keep his hand away from it. Some kind of trick, he thought; yet there'd been something in the way the man had asked that question that was a plain indication he was standing without a weapon. The gun had probably jounced loose coming out of that window. He said, "Over at Con Quilton's. Damn thing was gettin' too hair-triggered for safety."

For the space of three heartbeats they stared at each other. "Where's your horse?" the man said.

Crossing over Turk had noticed that one of the three at this rack, its companions, had not been tied. It stood a little apart with the reins over its neck. Having brought off one gamble, Turk now tried another. "Right behind you," he said, and knew before the words had half got out of his mouth that, this time, it wasn't going to work.

He didn't wait for the man to call him a liar. All he got was an impression of movement in the man's right shoulder but it was enough to send him into headlong action. Flame tearing out of the rifle's barrel almost blinded him. But he was into the man then, regardless of the pain, right fist driving straight and hard to the man's belly. The man staggered backward, doubled over, gasping. Turk's next blow almost unhinged the man's jaw.

Turk lunged for the pitching horses. He tripped and stretched his length with horses and lamplit buildings all scrambled together wheeling crazily around him. Waves of nausea rolled with him through a roaring sea of light streaked blackness and his left shoulder burned with all the agony of fire. He heard boots pounding toward him and someway clawed up out of the dust in time to see the frantic horses tear away with the ripped-loose tie rail. But the one with the reins up stood like a rock.

Big he was, a roan with the promise of plenty of bottom. He was trembling with excitement, one hoof pawing the ground. The whites of his eyes showed when Turk reached for him and his ears went back, his head twisting snakily. Turk's hand missed the reins and the horse reared, whirling, when Turk tried for the horn. Turk almost sobbed in frustration, but just when he figured he was caught afoot in this jackpot a man crashed out of the shadows behind him and the frightened horse spun and came plunging straight at Turk.

Swaying back, Turk grabbed and his hand hooked the horn. The horse was going like a twister when the seat of Turk's pants slicked into saddle leather.

# SEVEN

HER FATHER OFTEN declared with a little shake of the head that Rosarita cared nothing for the old Spanish customs and even less for traditions which she personally considered insufferable. "Traditions," he would remark with a long face put on for the benefit of shocked listeners, "frequently affect the Little Sister with a great deal of the same emotion which causes the brave bull to go after a red flannel cape."

Rosarita sometimes smiled when she heard but she had never denied the veracity of it. Born out of her time in a land shackled by custom she believed in the inalienable right of a woman to work out her own problems—and this in a day when the women of the Americans north of the border had not as yet dared even to dream of emancipation. She was a forthright young person with more than a little of the Moor about her look and sufficient courage and intelligence to live her life in accordance with her own set of values.

She knew where to find Turk's horse, for she had discovered it while returning just now from another of her unfruitful attempts to contact the elusive Jake. Which was how she had happened so providentially to be at hand when the Curly Bill—Fred White business had gotten Turk trapped on the porch by Wyatt Earp. After seeing his horse, which she had remembered from Silver Lake, it was the most natural thing in the world for her to bide there a while, just inside the ajar door, on the chance of again catching sight of the young gringo.

There was an earnestness, a wholesome lack of sophistication, about this Turkey Red which set him apart from most of these Americans so variously going about their life's work of piling up gringo dollars. He was perhaps as uncouth and rough as the others yet she had sensed in him a difference which inexplicably attracted her.

She looked covertly about her while speaking quietly to his horse and not seeing anything which alarmed her, swung lightly up into the saddle, totally unmindful of the amount of bare leg this displayed. She was at home in the saddle as most of her nationality, having practically lived in one all of her life. She had no difficulty with High Sailin. Reining him away from the rack she directed him uptown, taking in the sights and smells of this place as any Gypsy miss might.

Opposite the Can Can she wheeled him left with her knee, turning him south on Fourth, looking over the dwindling throngs of noisy people still abroad on the splintery planks of the walks. Why were the Americans, she wondered, always so loud? This boisterousness amounted almost to a national trait like their unquenchable lust for dollars. Even their songs—at least the ones you heard most in their cities—seemed to depend for popularity on catchiness and gusto. In her own land the peons preferred more leisurely airs and their ballads most frequently told of death and unrequited love. She thought that love was perhaps her people's main preoccupation. Possibly because they generally had so little else.

She swung left again on Tough Nut Street, going past the deserted shine of lamps seeping out of the front of the Arcade Hotel. Traffic was greatly reduced in this section. Only a few rumbling ore wagons churned up the dust and most of the buildings were dark, although here and there dim flickers of light still feebly showed from the cabins of miners scattered along the right slope.

She quickened High Sailin's pace with her knees, aware that women were not expected to be abroad here at this time and that any encounters she might chance to have would be with men whom liquor had put in an unruly frame of mind. She put a hand on her leg to make sure she had her knife. Naked steel worked a salutary effect on drunken gringos.

She turned north on Fifth, sending the brown into a dark and cluttered alley they would shortly bring her quietly to the trees she had asked Turk to wait in. Before she'd gone ten yards rifle sound slammed against the walls of the buildings and she bent forward, stopping the horse, listening with caught breath to the uproar beyond them. Was the redhead out there?

Boots, ahead of her, swept into a lifting run going streetward, and that seemed answer enough. The "star packers", as Jake called them, must have surrounded the rooming house and someway flushed him into the open. With a mounting sense of insecurity she heard a further racket of rifles and panic drove her heels against the brown gelding's ribs as her twist of the reins sent him through the black murk between buildings.

Before he came out of it a rushing thunder of hoofbeats tore through the shouts and the swearing, building into a wild drumming which fled south and went dim in a fading flutter of beaten pulsations. She stopped the brown horse in the alley's mouth, watching the sprinting shapes of men jerk loose knotted reins and pile into their saddles. There was still a tight constriction in her throat yet she breathed easier now, confident that Turk would elude them.

In any event it was in God's hands and she would go and light a candle beneath the Virgin's picture. Later, some time before morning, she would set out for Charleston and the corral of Frank Stilwell. Sooner or later that maddening Jake would turn up there; and who could say, since he had taken up with Bill, that this impetuous gringo of the flaming red hair might not also be found there?

Charleston was a collection of mud and frame shacks squatted down in a crotch of the San Pedro River some ten miles from Tombstone. The "town" was kept alive by a stamp mill and by the money Curly Bill's bunch squandered in its deadfalls. The place numbered at the most perhaps five hundred persons. The muddy river crawled half around it and ancient cottonwoods gave welcome shade. There was a deal of promiscuous shooting and someone got killed nearly every night but it was more noisy than wild when you stripped the brags away from it.

Jim Burnett was the big wheel at Charleston. "Justice of the Peace" he called himself but the only peace he had ever really valued was the piece of change he could shove in is pocket. He made up his own laws and enforced them at the business end of a double-barreled shotgun. He was a "card," to use Curly Bill's own word for him.

The place was trying its enthusiastic best to be more cussed then Tombstone. There wasn't a church within ten miles of its racket. There were dancehalls and gambling dives, one hotel, a schoolhouse and a vociferous pack of mangy dogs. And that was about the size of it.

Turk assimilated most of this listening to the loafers jawing and whittling around Frank Stilwell's. It seemed to him that his wounded shoulder took unconscionably long to mend but this was probably mostly due to all the blood he had lost on that wild ride from Tombstone. Nearly two weeks had passed before he was up and around. Stilwell told him he'd come in dead beat, out of his head and "talking a blue streak." Frank said half the town had turned out to get a whack at them Earps and had stood on their guns for two solid hours before going back to their whisky and women. According to Frank, that was considerable of a tribute. Turk guessed he meant to the Earps.

Frank had bedded Turk down in the hay of his

86

loft and by the time Turk was able to be up and around quite a few things had happened in that part of the country. Curly Bill had been tried and turned loose of White's killing and was someplace off in the hills gathering cattle. The county elections had been held and the law's tin stars had been reshuffled and, according to local tell, were apt to get reshuffled again by the look of it.

Charlie Shibell, over at Tucson, had been reelected sheriff by 47 votes. But there'd been some talk of fraud and the Earps had got the 104 votes from the San Simon district thrown out, which gave the sheriff's star to Earp's friend Bob Paul, who wasn't liked around Charleston. Curly Bill, it was hinted, had stuffed the San Simon ballot boxes; one of the names put down as a qualified voter being Hiram J. Gander which, upon investigation, was found to belong to a rooster owned by a Galeyville boarding house proprietor. Several cows, it was contended, had also voted. But Shibell had gone to the courts with his case and Wyatt Earp had stood off a mob of five hundred who had aimed to hang a gambler known as Johnny-Behind-the-Deuce. In spite of the thrown-out votes, however, popular Johnny Behan had kept his deputy's job, which suited the folks at Charleston right down to the cracked earth's grass roots.

Turk, not much interested in politics, let the most of this talk go in one ear and out the other. But Wyatt Earp, he learned, was still packing *his* badge and, being Federal, it was good all over the country. Another thing he heard was that rustlers had raided the Roman 4 and got off with 300 head of prime beef. He wished that he could have helped them.

But the old sap was stirring. The hole in his shoulder was pretty well scabbed over and he was anxious to earn his keep. He thought this morning that he would eat uptown and grinned at the tough look of himself thrown back by the water in the horse trough where he'd sluiced off his face and slicked back his shaggy mane. He guessed he'd ought to stake himself to a shave.

The broncs in the pen were all eating their heads off. He saw Frank with some other gents hunkered out front, passing gab and interminably whittling. Billy Clanton was one of them and Tom McLowery was there and old Jim Hughes with his jaw full of brown tobacco and a black browed hombre he reckoned was Jake Gauze. It was this black browed one that seemed to be doing the bulk of the talking. He broke off when Turk came up.

Frank Stilwell rasped his round cheeks and said, "Turkey, I guess you know Jake—he just rode in from Pine Mesa. Curly's over in Galeyville. Jake's fetched the word we're to all go over there day after tomorrer."

Jake Gauze, a sour lumpy toad of a man, threw Stilwell a riled look. "You don't have to tell the whole country about it."

"Hell, Turk's all right. He's with us," McLowery said—"you heard Bill take him on yourself."

Gauze backed around to his horse and got onto him. "The only stranger I'd trust is a dead one," he snarled and, raking his bronc with the steel, rode off.

"Crazy as a gopher," Hughes grunted, shaking his head.

McLowery stared after Gauze disgusted. "He'll give us trouble one of these days. All he thinks about is killin'."

Billy Clanton grinned. "He's got plenty of company. Curly's shore some riled over the way Wyatt buffaloed him that night of White's passin'."

"This place is too handy to Tombstone," Hughes said.

McLowery's lip curled. "Bill ain't forgetting that and I ain't either. Them goddam Earps is ridin' for a fall." He twisted his head around to scowl at Billy Clanton. "Got them fellers located?"

"Most of 'em," Clanton chuckled. "Give us another couple months and we'll have every waterhole from Mexico to the Muggyones. We kin ride from hell to breakfast an' never sight a hostile rifle."

He noticed Hughes looked at Turk and quit talking. Turk felt suddenly uncomfortable and couldn't think why he should. It was no skin off his nose if they wanted to grab all the waterholes. Far as he'd ever heard the Clantons and McLowerys were up-and-coming ranchers. Sure they probably drifted off a few loose cows when opportunity offered, but everyone did that. It was the way you got a brand built up. Nothing but common practice.

Turk's glance went beyond young Clanton just then and through the bars of the corral he saw the horse that had brought him from Tombstone that night and idly wondered what the animal was doing here. Frank Stilwell had told him he'd taken care of that horse, which he'd supposed to have meant the man had got rid of him. It kind of gave him a shock to see the horse still around. He was about to take it up with Frank when Jim Hughes allowed he'd better be getting himself an outfit. "And nothin' fancy," he said as Turk reluctantly got up. "Man could see that white shirt you're wearin' forty foot away at night." And Stilwell said, "I'll stake you to a bronc. Git yourself a rifle an' cartridges."

Frank pitched away his stick and got up and closing his knife dropped it into his pocket. After rummaging awhile he finally fetched out his purse. "If you're short I might lend you a couple of bucks, though Bunny won't like it."

He was always dragging "Bunny" into any talk that touched on finances. "I'll make out," Turk said. "This Bunny you're always bringin' up . . . Who is she—your wife?"

"No," Frank said while some of the others showed grins, "though I don't much misdoubt but what the thought has occured to her." He brushed the shavings off his pantlegs and looked up at Turk kind of sly like. "Speakin' of women, what you figurin' to do about yourn?"

"Mine!" Turk gasped. He stared in confusion and his face felt as though it must be twice as red as fire. "I don'tknow what you're talkin' about!"

"Might be you don't at that," Frank conceded— "she only come round while you was outen your head. Dang good thing Bunny wasn't here, by gollies—heavin' my bottle of horse medicine right through that new winder light! Said she'd brew up her own stuff, an' never left your side fer two whole days an' nights. Hell, I s'posed you knowed all about her."

"If he don't," Clanton chuckled, "he can find out quick enough. She's got her a job over at Jawbone Clark's." And McLowery said, "You better ease up on her careful. She give Milt Hicks a whole quart of forty-rod in the puss—bottle an' all. Said she didn't care for the way Milt was eyein' her!"

Hughes' head went back in a belly shaking guffaw as Turk wheeled away with burning ears. Frank called after him but Turk kept going; and Billy Clanton chortled, "Watch out fer that left leg, boy—she's got a knife up her garter."

Turk kicked a horse apple hell west and crooked. He felt wild enough to halfway consider whirling around and taking the whole works on. He knew well enough now what girl they were talking about and, while he was relieved in a way to know it hadn't been Holly, the thought of that dancer following him here sure gravelled him. It made him more embarrassed than ever to think of her up there pawing him over and him not even knowing a damn thing about it.

For perhaps a dozen strides he heard their whoops and guffaws and then he caught the squeak of a gate hinge and the lifting thud of hoof sound, but was too riled by then to look around and see what was happening. Like a door had been shut, all sound abruptly ceased.

In spite of himself, Turk slowed. These were Curly Bill's friends, and maybe he *was* acting the part of a chump to be showing resentment of their rough banter. Perhaps he was inclined to set too great a store on dignity; this hoorahing could be a first if rather boisterous indication of that which he prized most—acceptance, an acknowledgment that he was one of them. All his life he had wanted to belong, to be an accepted part of something; maybe it hadn't been his youth so much as temper which had barred him. At least their laughter wasn't hostile, as the look of that cross-grained Jake Gauze had been.

Turk stopped on this thought, and it came over him then with cold chills running through him that the silence around him had become too intense. He suddenly wanted to turn and was afraid to.

"Get off my horse!" the angry voice said flatly.

"Get out of the way or I'll run you down!"

That was Clanton. Not fooling, either. Something was winding up to happen back there, something coldly wicked, something ugly . . . Turk's head twisted.

Jim Hughes with all his whiskers, round-faced Frank and Tom McLowery made still and brittle shapes against the bars of the corral. Billy Clanton, about six lengths from the enclosure, was mounted on the horse that Turk had ridden here from Tombstone. Square in his way sat Wyatt Earp on another. He had a hand clapped to gun butt and his eyes gleamed like blue agate. "Get off," he said again, "and get that saddle off."

Clanton's look was black with anger but he got down and pulled his gear off. Earp's boots struck the ground and he walked up and put a rope around the blue roan's neck. He spun abruptly, yanking Clanton's pistols from their leathers. "You won't be needing these for a while. I'll be leaving them in the road for you on the other side of the bridge."

They stood glaring at each other through the frozen breath-locked quiet. "If I thought," Earp said at last, "you were the one that stole this horse from me I'd settle your hash right now."

Those were fighting words and the lash of his stare left no doubt in Turk's mind that he meant them to be so, yet nobody moved or even batted an eyelash.

With a grimace of contempt Earp swung into his saddle. He sat shortening the rope he had put on the roan and was turning the one he was on around when Billy Clanton snarled on an outrush of breath. "Next time it won't be that bronc we'll git but *you!*"

Earp gave him a long hard look. "Any time," he said thinly. "Make your play whenever it suits you and fetch all the friends you've a mind to."

He lifted his reins and cantered off up the trail.

For a couple of moments no one said anything.

Turk felt mortified for them, almost ashamed to have seen the man face these boys down. All his thoughts were in turmoil, his sense of fitness shaken, his scale of values threatening to crumble before his eyes. Were these Bill's friends that suddenly looked so much like coyotes?

He heard whiskered Jim Hughes let his breath out and watched him slump emptily down on his boot heels. McLowery wiped a hand against his pants and looked at Stilwell. Clanton slammed around and loosed a spate of rough talk. Frank said, "Mebbe Bill was right to shift headquarters over to Galeyville."

Clanton raked Frank with the edge of mean eyes. "Just because—"

But Turk had heard all he cared to. He felt too let-down and smothery-miserable to want to listen to any more of these fellows' jawing. He turned away like a man on his first trip with stilts and headed blindly uptown, bitter-squirming with the knowledge of what one kill-crazy badge toter could do to four of Bill's friends without even raising his voice.

# EIGHT

IT SURE GAVE him something to chew on.

By the time he'd got up to where he could see Cruikshank's barber pole his thoughts had swung around to viewing things considerably closer, like the almighty narrow margin with which he had come out of that deal himself. Only for walking off like he had, with the boisterous racket of their ragging hooting after him, he'd probably now—like that horse—be on his way back to Tombstone! It had been God's own mercy Wyatt Earp hadn't noticed him.

He thought maybe he'd be wise to change his mind about that shave. This red fuzz along his cheeks and the bend of his jaws wasn't near as hard to take as the prospect of feeling a rope around his neck. He had just been plain lucky and that was all there was to it. He thought now he might have been a shade harsh in his judgment of Clanton and McLowery and of Frank and old Jim. Maybe there was more to living than things seen bold in blacks and whites. Maybe there was gray shades, too, that tended to get lost most times in issues more apparent.

Turk was a little astonished to find the way his mind could slip around to other views. Before he'd come to Jawbone Clark's the most of the gimp had worked out of his legs and the turn of his thoughts had taken on sharper focus. Maybe Curly Bill's friends had damn good reason for letting Wyatt Earp tongue-lash them like he had; it was possible Bill's own orders had stood in the way of their natural reactions. There might be wheels within wheels he didn't know anything about.

He was willing to leave it at that for the moment. He wasn't even riled now at the thought of Rosarita taking so much on herself and brazenly following him down here. But on one thing he stood firm: If Bill had moved his head-quarters like that talk back there had hinted, it hadn't been on account of he was scairt of that damned marshal. Turk knew this man too well for that. Curly Bill wasn't scairt of anything!

Turk had been aiming to go and have a talk with that dancer but decided to put it off. He bent his steps toward the Mercantile and, still with his thoughts whirling around pretty free like, was passing the Eagle Hotel when a man said so close he caught a whiff of his breath, "Jumpin' craw-fishes, boy—git hold of the bit an' pull up here a moment!"

Turk sent a hand toward his holster, then dropped it, looking sheepish. It was Tex Willbrandt talking, and he'd been doing his share of drinking by the weavery way he stood there.

"Hi, Tex," Turk said, and the rusty-haired man grinned, beckoning him over beside the porch where he had managed to anchor bony shoulders against the rail.

"Been lookin' fer you," he grumbled, peering around and lowering gruff voice to a conspiratorial whisper. "Bill's got a job fer you," he said, loudly belching. He got a handful of Turk's gambler's shirt in his fist and wabbly-legged led him around the side of the building. He was sucking on one of those everlasting peppermints but the reek of cheap whisky was so all-fired potent the lozenge smell had hard work getting through. He loosed a couple of hiccups and tugged Turk, stooping, under the alamosas' branches. "Wantcha t' meet two of my buddies," he wheezed and, at a table set back in the sundappled shadows, Turk saw the riled faces of two men looking at him.

Tex introduced them as Charlie Thomas and John Ringo. They were dressed like most of Bill's bunch in puncher garb, and both had guns strapped around their middles and wore big hats and had bright spurs on their expensive looking boots. Thomas would have looked right at home with Linderstrom's outfit, having the earmarks of a gun hand; but the other fellow, Ringo, was something else again.

Turk was plenty impressed, having heard more than a little about John Ringo. He had the face of a discouraged preacher and about as large a reputation as the Earps' friend Doc Holliday. He was an educated man, Turk had heard, and one of the real he-cata-wampuses of Curly Bill's outfit. It was said he drank to drown a secret sorrow and was related to the Youngers.

Turk gave them the kind of nod Curly favored. Ringo grunted. Charlie Thomas just stared. Tex said, "Turkey, Bill wants you to come a-runnin'— wants you over there to Galeyville quick as you kin git there. Ain't that right, gents? Didn't—"

"Another of his grandstand plays," Ringo snorted, "like plugging Fred White right under Earp's nose."

Turk would have had to been green as Sulphur Valley grass not to have caught the biting sarcasm of that; and he looked at Ringo, surprised and half minded to put the man straight, only Tex, with a fleeting glance at Turk's face and looking suddenly almost sober, said too quick for him, "Aw, you know Bill never meant nothin' like that, John. You heard what Earp said. That gun went off accidental. White had holt of the barrel—"

"And you never thought that was funny?" Contempt twisted Ringo's handsome face. "You've watched him practice that roll by the hour, same as I have. I say he handed that gun to White butt first."

"You're just sore," Tex said, "account of—"

"You bet I'm sore," Ringo growled, and went back to his drinking. "No curly-haired bastard is going to shortchange me!"

Tex caught hold of Turk's arm and pulled him away from them. "C'mon boy," he said, "I got somethin' out here t' show you." He led Turk around to the back of the hotel and there was High Sailin, standing on his reins and with a new saddle on him looking chipper as forty jay birds. The horse let out a little whicker and came up and nuzzled Turk's shoulder.

Willbrandt grinned. "Cripes, you *are* tickled, ain'tcha! Bill allowed you would be. You'll prob'ly find him at Babcock's bar. You better git right over there. I got the idea this deal is important."

Galeyville was a boom silver camp strewn along the damp rim of a dark stony mesa thrust out of an ash and sycamore tangle that was Turkey Creek Canyon on the San Simon side of the Cherrycow Mountains. The place had been named for John H. Galey who'd struck oil in the East and was still taking ore from the discovery mine. Since no usable wagon roads were available and transportation was reduced to what a fellow could pack out on burros, he had put in a smelter. The main section of the community flanked the rim of this sawed-flat hill, with the dives and the stores all facing the bottoms across the broad width of what passed for the street. All, that is, but Nick Babcock's bar which was the biggest of the lot and had the whole other side of the town to itself with its back side squatted right above the gurgling creek.

There was a live oak growing out in front of Nick's place and under its shade Bill was comfortably ensconced in an old fashioned rocker. He had a bottle of beer in one big fist and his six-shooter barking from each jump of the other.

He was picking off a line of empty whisky containers set up on their necks in the middle of the road. Quite a crowd had collected and Turk could see the glass fly every time Bill squeezed trigger—he was sure suspending business in that dive across the way. While he was poking fresh loads in the cylinder, one of those gents standing nearest cried, "Yippee—watch this!" and, grabbing out his own iron, drove a .45 slug right through his own left leg. He yelled like a stuck pig while all the rest of the hyenas laughed fit to kill themselves—all but Curly.

He reared out of his chair with a disgusted grunt. "This yere roadagent's spin ain't fer clowns an' damn fools! Takes a sharp sense of timin' an' you got to know how to do it. Put your finger in the guard," he growled, "with the gun held upside down, butt forward." He proceeded to demonstrate, pinwheeling the heavy Colt's around the hub of his finger and banging away every time the barrel levelled. When he got done there wasn't a whole bottle out there.

Turk watched him punching out the spent ones, replacing them with live shells thumbed from his belt. Bill's glance, coming up and around, crossed Turk's face and he put the big pistol away with a nod. Turk took this to mean that their talk was to be private.

He rode on, picking his way through the still-grabbing tatters of the dispersing crowd and sliding down from his horse in front of Nick's batwings. He let go of the reins and pushed through the weather-grayed half-leaf doors, backing up against a wall while his eyes, narrowed now, compensated for the dimness after all that outside glare. The place was practically empty. A drowsy looking gent with his shirt off back of the bar was trying to entice a botfly to light enough to hit him.

Curly Bill came in and Turk followed him to the bar—the longest one he had ever seen, painted black as a coffin and crisscrossed and splintered with the tracks of old battles. Bill twisted his head and gave him a grin. "You name it, kid."

"Whatever you want'll be good enough for me."

Bill reared back and slapped the bar. "Hear that, Kelly?" he whooped, laughing. "We're goin' to make a real hand outa this 'un!"

The apron tried a grin for size. If flapped a little around the edges but Turk didn't care and reckoned Bill never noticed. It felt like coming home to be around him; good to hear the boom of that rollicking laughter. As he had in the past, he again stored up in his mind how Bill stood, how he carried himself, that bold and confident roll of his eyes. Turk would have given five years of his life to be like him; and Bill told the barkeep, "A bottle of your best and a pair of clean glasses, for my friend Turkey Red has rode a long way to git here." And he flashed Turk a wink.

Kelly set them on the bar. "Fetch 'em along," Bill said, and Turk packed them in the back room after him, trying to give to his walk the same roll Bill's had. He put the stuff on a table while Bill was shutting the door.

Pulling up a chair Bill sat down across from Turk. He knocked the neck off the bottle and filled both their glasses. "Here's mud in your eye!" Bill tossed his off and, putting down the glass, settled both elbows on the table with a confidential nod. "How well do you know that old goat at Roman 4?"

Bill was like that, one minute talking like a grubline rider and the next using words that had you fighting your hat to get a line on their meaning. "You mean Reubusch?" Turk said, stalling.

Bill filled up their glasses again, and still with that half smile quirking his mouth corners, nodded.

Turk tried to hold his voice level and speak as casual as Bill had, but the craving to get back at that bunch for setting the law on him was too strong for containment. "We could snatch that old coot blind!" he cried.

Bill pushed his glass around, edging its bottom into the rings on the table. He didn't seem to have heard Turk. "How much store does he put on that fluff he's got? Would he put up hard cash to git her back, do you reckon?"

Turk stared like he couldn't believe his own ears. "You mean . . . Holly?" he gulped.

Bill looked right back at him and his eyes, of a sudden, did not seem quite so twinkly. Then he was nodding again, big and sure; the Bill Turk remembered. "You been around there some, ain't you? How'd that pair strike you? Reckon he'd go fer five thousand?"

Turk couldn't think in that first stunned surprise; he could only sit there, jaw hanging, like he didn't have all his buttons.

"It wouldn't be so tough," Bill grinned. "But would he go for it? Would he go to five g's to git her back in his bed?"

102

Turk could feel the sweat cracking out against his collar. He couldn't get the tongue down off the roof of his mouth.

The upper lids of Bill's eyes kind of tightened a little, the creases deepening at their corners. "You ain't sick, kid, are you?"

"Gosh, Bill . . . I dunno," Turk said.

"You don't know what—if you're sick or if he'd go fer it?"

Turk tried to pull himself together. He reckoned Bill was figuring to work this deal for him, to square Turk's account with Roman 4 and at the same time to pick up a few bucks for his brother. Turk tried to put the uglier side of it out of his mind. It hadn't occurred to Bill, of course, how Turk might feel about Holly; and it wasn't anything that he could talk to Bill about. Loose one breath of suspicion and a girl's good name was gone.

Turk squirmed in his chair, hardly knowing what to say but all too keenly aware that he had got to say something. And then some other things crossed his mind and he saw he'd got to convince Bill that there were less risky ways. He shook his head. "Too much chance of somethin' goin' haywire. Town like this . . ." He shook his head more emphatically. "I don't expect in the first place we could ever git hold of her—"

"You needn't fret about that."

"And besides," Turk said, desperate, "while I don't mind runnin' off a few steers or horses, it would sure go plumb again' my grain to get mixed up with—"

"You won't git mixed up with it," Bill pushed

Turk's glass at him. "She's already grabbed."

The place got so still you could hear the birds in those trees beyond the window and the scuff of boots going past outside. "Hell," Curly laughed, "you don't need to look so damn solemn. Drink up —time's awasting," he said, shoving back in his chair and thrusting his legs out. He stretched burly arms, yawning. "A well setup piece . . . I guess he'll kick in, all right."

Turk wasn't half hearing him. He had to lick his lips twice to get the words out. "When'd you grab her?"

"Couple or three weeks ago. You don't need to worry, she ain't damaged none—yet.  Most of the boys don't even know she's here, and . . ."

Turk was back in Tucson at that place on South Meyer, seeing Holly's face again, hearing her say, "You crazy damn fool—" when he'd bragged he'd join Bill. The vision blurred and then cleared with him frozen to that walk on Allen Street in Tombstone, staring at Ruebusch's mottled features, seeing the wild shine of his half crazy eyes. Turk knew what the end of that question was now; and there was a kind of gale whirling around the inside of him and his thoughts wouldn't track, but he understood now what had pushed Ruebusch at him. The goddamn chump thought his wife had run off with Turk!

Bill was looking at him, curious. Turk pushed a hand across his damp cheeks. A sick emptiness was inside him and he caught up the refilled glass and drained it, gagging on the stuff and having to fight to get his breath but someway wishing he'd had to fight longer.

He wanted mightily to tell Bill Ruebusch wouldn't pay. But he knew he couldn't do that, scared of what might happen. Pretty near anything could happen in a place like this. He couldn't even tell Bill how he felt himself about Holly—or could he? Was there some way he could enlighten Bill without revealing all?

If there was, Turk couldn't find it. Nor dared he ask where they were holding her.

Bill pushed to his feet, stood considering him a moment. "You better git some rest, kid. Got a heap of ridin' to do in the mornin.' We'll talk of this again."

But Turk couldn't leave it there. Confused, uncertain, horribly afraid for her, he got out of his chair, catching Bill's arm as Bill turned toward the door. "What if he won't pay?"

Bill's head came around, eyes quartering over Turk's face like steel fingers. "You got any reason to think he won't?"

Turk's glance fell away with the hopelessness of it; and he stood there knowing his mouth was open and not finding any words with Bill seeming so still and terribly strange of a sudden. It was like he wasn't the same person.

Then the frozen rigidity was gone and Bill grinned. "You better hit the hay, kid. Way you look now you couldn't ride nothin' wilder than a wheel-chair. What's happened to your gun?"

Turk's hand went like a sleepwalker to his waist, then he remembered. "Lost it," he muttered, "gettin' out of a window."

"And ain't got the price of another, eh?" Bill sloshed a hand in his pocket, flipped a gold piece at Turk and said, "Go over to Harbaker's an' git yourself heeled. Kelly'll fix you up with a bed. I'll see you later."

# NINE

Turk felt plain sick.

How long he stood eyeing the closed door after Bill left he never knew. Time had no meaning. Nothing had meaning but the fact of Holly's capture; that she was somewhere in this town and had been here, Bill's prisoner, for more than two weeks. At first it hadn't seemed possible, but now that his shocked mind had had more chance to grasp it he was able to see how it tied in with other things, like Ruebusch jumping him and that rustler's raid that had taken 300 head of cattle from Ruebusch's ranch—that was when they'd grabbed her, probably.

He picked up the double eagle that had rolled beneath the table and thrust it absently in his pocket. He could imagine her feelings, the awful strain she must have been under, the desperation of knowing she was finished with Roman 4. Ruebusch, feeling as he did, would never take her back now—or would he?

The man had obviously seen or been told something which had caused him to distrust Turk's relations with the girl. Else, when she'd disappeared, he would not have been so quick to believe she'd gone to Turk, as the man plainly did. No, Turk thought morosely, Ruebusch would have washed his hands of her by now.

In the present confused state of his emotions Turk entirely overlooked the man's most likely reaction, the natural desire for revenge which he would almost certainly be nursing, a desire bound to have been whetted by their recent clash in Tombstone. All Turk could think of in this moment was that he'd got to find Holly and someway get her out of Bill's hands and away from here. Bill would shortly—if indeed he hadn't already—be dispatching a demand for her ransom.

Turk could understand Bill's place in this. It was obvious. Bill couldn't help himself. He'd been trapped in this deal just as surely as Turk was. Some of his bunch—guys like Thomas and Gauze —had grabbed the girl with an eye to what her husband would give to get her back safe and sound, and had probably told Bill he'd better ask for five thousand. It was as simple as that—and what could Bill do? His control of this bunch must be a delicate business; they'd never stand for him turning her loose without a payoff . . .

This brought other considerations to Turk's mind. Like what the bunch would do if Turk himself succeeded in freeing her—the spot it would put Bill in, and himself.

He went out the back door and walked around to High Sailin and got his shell belt and holster and headed across the road, looking for

108

Harbaker's, which he reckoned would be either a gun shop or mercantile.

It turned out to be a general store with a case and gun rack off at the left rear behind the leather goods and horse furniture. Turk counted it lucky he still had a few bucks of his own and bought, first of all, a dark blue shield-fronted shirt and a black neckerchief to go with it. He also paused to look at some hats but finally decided to make the one he had do till he was in greater funds.

Picking his way through the saddles and stacked blankets and the head stalls and harness hanging from pegs, he went over to the gun case. There he purchased a single action Colt's .45 after trying out several for heft and balance. He slipped it into his scuffed holster and got a box of cartridges although he still had a few in the loops of his belt. Made him feel kind of mean, in a way, arming himself with Bill's money for a project which, if he could bring it off, would practically amount to doublecrossing Bill.

Back at Babcock's bar, after he'd put up his horse, he braced Kelly about the chances for a bed. There was a balcony built out around two sides of the room and there were doors opening off it which he reckoned most likely was where the beds would be. Kelly, twisting his neck, took a look up the stairs and Turk, turning also, saw Bill coming down them.

"Fix him up," Bill said and, coming over, stopped beside Turk, giving him a poke in the ribs with his elbow. "See you got your pistol," he grinned, "an' what's this—a new shirt? Good idea," he nodded, approving Turk's choice of colors. He tossed the barkeep a key. "I sent a man off with the news to our friend. Mebbe he won't be feelin' so high an' mighty now. We'll show him, by God, who's runnin' this country! Outside of right around here, who ever heard of old man Rue- busch? But they've all heard of me, kid—clean up to Washin'ton!"

His laugh rang around the walls of the room and came back to give him a kind of pat on the shoulder. It was the truth, though, Turk thought; and then his eyes narrowed down as the batwings flapped and Jake Gauze came into the place. The same perpetual beard stubble darkened his cheeks and the high flat face, as he came to a stop, showed a sullen resentment as his glance locked with Turk's. And then his look jumped at Bill. "What's he doin' here?"

Bill showed his gold tooth. "You got the deal all lined up?"

"I ain't talkin' in front of no blabbermouth kid!"

Turk, flushing, started forward. Bill's arm hauled him back; and Bill's elbow, digging Turk's ribs, fetched a grunt that was lost in Bill's laugh as Bill said, "Ever see a more roundabout guy in your life, kid? Jake's so damn careful he has to git a drink from the dipper! Haw haw haw!"

Jake glared, swung around and went stomping out.

"Hell," Bill said, "now he's mad again, dammit. You go on an' ketch that shut-eye—Kelly'll give you a shout when we're ready to ride." He slapped Turk's shoulder and wheeled off after Gauze.

"Bad actor, that feller," Kelly said, shaking his

head. "Killed the Brayton boys here in a flare-up last week—meaner than a centipede with chilblains."

"Speakin' of centipedes," Turk said, "You got anythin' I can chew on?"

"You can hev a couple of these," Kelly grunted, setting a plate of picked-over sandwiches on the bar. They didn't look very fresh but Turk bit into one anyway, reckoning they'd stay his hunger till he found time for something better. He put five of them away and then got a beer to slosh them down with. "You don't seem to have much business," he remarked.

"Little early yet," Kelly said with a sniff. "When that smelter bunch knocks off we'll hev three aprons busy." He waved a hand at the stairs. "Better kitch that sleep now if you aim to; goin' to get a mite noisy come lamp lightin' time."

When Turk still stood there, the barkeep said, again waving at the stairs, "Just take any of them rooms that's empty," and went back to polishing glasses.

Turk climbed the stairs and pushed open the first door he came to, tossing the paper-sacked shirt on the rumpled blanket-covered bed that left just enough space to bypass it to the window, which Turk went to as soon as he had pushed shut the door. He didn't see much that looked to offer any help. There were trees outside but none he could get into; their roots were in the creek and it was too far to risk a drop.

Turk didn't like it. The narrow six-by-ten cell—which was all it really amounted to—gave him a feeling of being trapped, yet he knew if he tried to go somewhere else now the move would be regarded with suspicion. If he was to help Holly at all he would have to proceed with a great deal of caution, because he sure wasn't going to help anyone dead. And he could be dead damned quick if he was caught in this caper.

He pulled off the white shirt he'd been wearing since Silver Lake and, regretting there wasn't a washbowl or water in the room, got into the blue one, more than half minded to go out and hunt up a barber. He realized he was deliberately trying to put off thinking about Holly and, though he was all tangled up in his mind about her, he reckoned a real man would face it.

He didn't know what ailed him really. Everything seemed to be all mixed up and nothing appeared to be the way he'd always had it figured. His whole scale of values looked to be busted wide open and even Curly Bill, by God, that Turk would have swore was unchangeable as rock, didn't seem like he had when Turk was drawing down his wages at Ruebusch's Roman 4.

He put his coat back on and his hat and went down the stairs.

Kelly, back of the bar, was still yawning on his glasses, and there was a couple of fellows with their elbows hooked over it and one of them was Thomas that he had met with John Ringo that morning outside Charlie Tarbell's Eagle Hotel at Charleston. He was so narrow between the ears Turk guessed he could look through a keyhole with both eyes at once.

"I'm goin' to scout up a barber,"Turk said with

a nod at the barkeep, "and see about gettin' myself a soak in his tub."

"Across the street," Kelly waved, "about ten doors down."

Turk had to wait his turn at the tub so he let the fellow shave him to help pass the time. After the barber had put powder on his face with a kid's-size feather duster, Turk guessed he might as well go ahead and roach his mane while he was at it. "Reckon you're kind of new around here," the barber said after he'd run through the most of his jokes. "You don't look like a miner. Guess you're figurin' to latch on with Curly Bill's bunch."

Turk let it ride. The barber frowned but kept snipping. He wet Turk's hair down with some fancy smelling stuff which he shook out of an opaque bottle. When he pulled off the striped sheet and Turk had paid him, he said, "You kin go along in there now if you want to."

Turk felt a heap better when he got out of the tub. The sun was heeling low in the west, putting an edging of color around the knobs of the Three Sisters and a few of those nearer peaks and deepening and darkening the shapes of some of the others. He was remembering the key Bill had tossed the barkeep and beginning to do some tall wondering about it.

Kelly, when he got back, was setting out some fresh sandwiches and Turk helped himself to a couple as he passed. The narrow-faced Thomas and his hard-eyed companion were still anchored to the foot rail nursing a pair of whiskies. Thomas said, "Red, I want you to know Charlie Snow."

And to Snow: "This is the jigger that put that winder in Fanshaw."

Turk didn't care for the tone of that last nor for the look he got from Snow's brightening glance but he gave them a Curly Bill nod and went on up the stairs. Night was closing down fast and there was something he wanted to do before Kelly got around to lighting the lamps.

He heard more guys coming in and pushed open his door, closing it again without entering the room, standing there listening to the mutter of voice sounds, concealed from the men down below by the overhang. Very cautiously then he tried the next door and the door just beyond, trying to locate the one Bill had used that key on. The third door wouldn't give and Turk put an ear against it, twisting the knob again and hearing with quickened breathing the faint shreak of springs beyond it.

Was this the one? Was this where they had her?

He caught the pad of bare feet moving around inside and his heart got to thumping and a mounting excitement almost choked off his breathing. He was totally unprepared for the door's sudden opening and lurched forward, off balance, almost impaling himself on the cold steel of the knife the girl held in front of her blanket-wrapped shape.

He stumbled back in alarm; and that was when he realized the scurvy deal he'd got from fate. With that window back of the girl he couldn't make out her features but even in this gloom he knew it wasn't Holly's hair.

114

# TEN

THE ROOM LOOKED very much like the one he'd
changed his shirt in except there wasn't any
blanket on the bed; it was around the girl. She
clutched it to her with the hand that held the
knife, pulling him away from the door with the
other one, sending it shut with the push of a foot.
Now the light from the window fell across her face
and the look of her eyes, still surprised, revealed
pleasure. And the edges of something else which
eluded him.

"So you have followed me here, Turkey Red."
She spoke softly, almost wonderingly, more as
though the words were for herself than for him. "I
am glad," she said simply; and moved back a little,
away from him. "If you will step outside a
moment I'll get into my—"

Turk's harsh growl cut her off. "I didn't come
here to talk." Anger was beginning to work up
through the shock of his disappointment and he
glared at her, forgetful in his suspicion, of what
this girl had done for him. What he had seized on

115

in the confusion of his teeming thoughts was that she was turning up too often for coincidence.

A concerned look twisted her gamin features and she said quickly, "Your shoulder hurts?"

"Hell with my shoulder!" But he was remembering now those two nights and those days she'd spent nursing him through that delirium in Frank's loft, and it made him look an ungrateful cur; but he went on with it anyway, determined in his baffled rage to get this business of her settled anyhow. "I want to know why you been follerin' me around!"

"But I haven't," she said; and then her face changed its shape and she clutched her blanket tighter with scorn coming into the flash of her eyes. "Hoh!" she said, flinging back her black hair and staring him up and down with thinned lips. "What gives you this idea, eh? You got poco dinero—a lot of money, maybe? Many horses?"

"Never mind," Turk growled. "I don't want you follerin' me. I got troubles enough without you mixin' into them!"

She looked at him carefully. Gave a hard little laugh. She swapped her hold on the blanket and with no other warning came straight for him with the knife.

Turk had never heard of The Woman Scorned but he was certainly in the way of collecting a first-hand sample of some very stormy reactions. He got a glimpse of bare flesh as she let go of the blanket and after that he was much too taken up with trying to keep from getting skewered to have any time for sight seeing.

He tried to get hold of her wrist and very nearly

116

got his throat slit. He backed away from her, panting. She followed, eyes watching for a chance to get at him. The flats of his shoulders hit the wood of the door.

It was the end of the line. He couldn't go any farther without pulling it open. He couldn't do that without twisting around and he dared not take his eyes off her that long. He said, "For Christ's sake, Rita!" and sweat dripped off his chin.

Her eyes were like live coals shining at him, the measured slap of her feet a voodoo beat from the jungle. He glimpsed the plunging glint of the knife and winced away from it, dragging his back down the scrape of the door as the gleaming steel sheathed its length in the upper panel.

Before she could yank it loose he had hold of her. She fought with the silent fury of a wildcat. To get under that blade he'd gone into a squat and now he had no chance to pull out of it. The advantage lay with her and she used it, angrily driving a knee into his chest. She grabbed a handful of hair and banged his head against the door. He got both arms around her legs and strove desperately to throw her. It wrenched her grip from the knife. She went down on her back and it shook the breath out of her.

This apparently enraged her. She grew wilder than ever. She slammed a knee into his face and the whole room went black and rocked in a shuddering blaze of bursting lights. When he dragged up his hands something hit him in the stomach. Half crazy with pain he clouted her then and when he heard her cry out he clouted her again. She fell away from him, limp; and in that cessation of hostilities he heard boots on the stairs.

He was too sick to get up. Even desperate as he was with their approach he couldn't make it. He heard the boots split up as though they moved in two directions, and one portion of this sound was obviously coming nearer. Turk did what he could. "Get away from there—" he growled through the rasp of his breathing. "Can't a man have a gut ache without the whole camp gettin' in on it?"

He heard the boots mill to a standstill, caught the mutter of whispers. Someone laughed nastily. The boots reluctantly moved off down the stairs and, outside, a lift of wind whirled through the massed foliage, tossing a clack of branch ends against the back wall of the building.

When the tension finally went out of him, Turk felt weak as a dish rag. He would have killed anyone who came through that door then. It was a sobering thought and he considered it, trying to dig up the cause for such a feeling and wondering where this crazy streak was taking him. Then it was the girl's queer stillness that was troubling him and he stared to push himself up, shamed and regretful and halfway worried he might have hurt her.

He couldn't see why these things always happened to him; and in the confused tangle of his bitter thoughts the frustration that was in him cried out against the uncaring way fate was using him. He'd never asked for much of anything. Just the chance to be a part of what went on around him, to have a feeling of belonging—his own small share of that respect men gave to others.

He shoved up onto an elbow and in the graying gloom saw the girl's eyes flutter open. She knocked the arm off from under him. He came down onto her like a sack of dropped feed, his chin jarring into a firm but yielding surface. A whimpering cry rushed out of her, but instead of striking back at him she locked both arms around his neck; and abruptly their mouths had got someway tight together and he could feel the fierce way she was straining her shape against him. He felt the thump of her heart; and her lips, responsive now with passion, made him increasingly excited; and amazed to find himself liking this—and kind of half angered too—he pulled away from her, struggling to get onto his feet.

She whispered something he didn't catch, and said, "Is this how the gringos . . ." letting the rest of it go, reaching up for him. "Turkey—now!" she cried in a stifled voice; and aghast, he whirled to his feet. Embarrassed, revolted, he stumbled blindly toward the door, hardly conscious of what he was doing, knowing only the need to get out and away from her. Ought to be horsewhipped, his seething mind told him, rolling around with this half-growed stumpet and Holly, a prisoner, not a rope's cast away!

*Not a rope's cast away . . .*

The words plunged through him like stones through a millrace, rooting him there, rigid stiff with eyes staring and the split-up sound of those boots noisily tramping across the whirl of his thoughts.

The blood pounded into his throat, almost

119

choking him with the conviction of Holly's nearness. And then his shifting glance picked up the haft of that knife skewered into the door where the girl had driven it. He spun round to see her standing with the blanket clutched about her, winklessly watching him.

Hating himself he went back to her. Led her over to the bed and sat down with her. It turned him sick to see that expression of hope breaking through the confusion which had stopped her tongue's clatter, to feel that cold little hand closing round his own. But it was the only chance he could see. He had to do it. He couldn't get that key from the barkeep himself.

Her hand squeezed his. "Take me with you. I am strong. I can ride. I will cook for you and sometimes at night when the moon is low I will bring my gifts through the shadows of your blanket. Even though it pleases you to beat me . . . and I will not ask for the marriage."

In spite of everything it touched him. Her heightened color, the strange mingling of shyness with pride in the way the words came out of her, almost weakened his resolve until his mind threw back at him the coincidence of her turning up at Tombstone, Charleston and now here at Babcock's, and the things Arch had said at Silver Lake to Flack about her. He pulled his hand away impatiently.

She must have sensed what he was thinking. At least she told him she'd been hunting for her brother—a half-brother, really, the son of her father's first wife, it appeared; a bad lot who had caused the old man much worry. "But he cannot see it," she urged softly. "His poor heart is breaking because this nogood has gone away from him and taken up with others like himself who rob and cheat and kill defenseless people. So for a while I go with the *chalanes*—the Gypsy horse dealers who travel everywhere, and dance for my keep like any *gitana*—gypsy; and I find this one and follow him, but it is all of no use. He laughs at me when I speak of our father and calls me a bad name." She spread her hands helplessly. "There is no more I can do."

Crazy as they sounded her words carried conviction. But they didn't explain how she had known he was crouched on that porch back of Tombstone, or how she'd found him at Charleston and now happened to be here. He mentioned this, and even in the near dark of this tree-thickened gloom he could feel the surprise that looked out of her face.

"But I saw you in Tombstone—I saw you come onto the veranda to hide. And I did not know where you went when you left. I heard the guns, but you were gone—all of them were; and I had not yet talked with my brother. It was natural I should go to Charleston. The corral of "Pancho Stealwell," as my people call him, is a place where all the time these hunted ones go for fresh horses and information. I feel sure my brother will go there. And perhaps, I think, you may come there too, so I take your horse—"

"You took High Sailin?"

"How else would he get there?"

Turk was shaken but not convinced. Perhaps he did not wish to be—for hadn't Tex Willbrandt of the peppermint breath given the impression Curly Bill had sent High Sailin over there? Scowling, Turk said, "Your talk's sure improved; you wrangle our lingo a heap better than I do!"

She shrugged, not answering, when Turk got up and took a turn about the room. She pulled the blanket a little closer around her shoulders, her glance following him. "I can help you—" she began; and he came back, saying, "Maybe you can."

His expression looked worried and a little bit nervous. "There's a girl in this place . . . about your size and damn pretty; and they're holdin' her —Bill's bunch—figurin' to make her husband kick in with a pile of jack. He's a rancher over near Benson. I happen to know he won't pay them a cent. I've got to get her out of here—you want to help me with that?"

For a long breath she stared at Turk without moving. Then she pushed back her hair and got up off the bed. She went over by the window with the blanket pulled tight around the curves of her figure and stood looking into the deepening dusk. "Who is this woman, eh? What is she to you?"

"I just told you she was married—"

"And what has that to do with it!"

"It's her looks," Turk said, trying hard to explain it. "Hair that's the color of a field of ripe wheat—and that ain't all. You ought to be able to figure what'll happen if these brush jumpers don't git their hands on that money! The girl's a lady— Ruebusch's wife! The feller I used to ride for."

She showed a little more concern. "He is your friend, this one?"

"I . . ." Turk frowned. "I wouldn't hardly say that—but it ain't him I'm worried about. It's just that . . ." He let the rest go. He said, "I ain't blamin' Bill—" and stopped again, struck with the futility of attempting to put into words an impulse he didn't half understand himself. It wasn't that he imagined Holly might have been trying to find him, or that he still had any hope of ever persuading her to go off with him, but some way or other he just couldn't help feeling tied up with her troubles. In spite of all that had happened he still couldn't get Willow Springs out of his head.

She rasped a bare foot across the splintery boards and turned around to eye him unreadably. "What do you want me to do?"

"Barkeep's got a key to her room—that guy Kelly," Turk said, looking more hopeful. "You ought to be able to wean it away from him. You could tell him she's sick, that she wants you to come in there, that when you find out what's wrong you could maybe fix—"

"When I get this key, what are you going to do then?"

"I'll find some way to slip her out," Turk growled. "We'll put her on a horse and git her headed for Benson."

"She is prettier than me, this woman?"

"Hell, she's the most—" He stopped and looked at her more carefully. "What difference does that make?"

"Are you not afraid that someone else may run off with her?"

Turk rubbed a hand across his jaw and chewed his lip. This kid had a head on her shoulders. The possibility hadn't occurred to him, but he could see that she was right and he would have to keep his eyes peeled.

"Glad you thought of that," he grunted. "Guess I'll have to stick with her a ways. Have to scout up some clothes and she'll need a horse, too. We'll have to hide that hair. Reckon you could darken her face up a little?"

Rita said, "I will take care of her."

"Good girl," Turk nodded. "You go ahead and git that key."

She said, "I will have to put some clothes on," and Turk, with his cheeks turning hot as a stove lid, went over and glared out of the window while she got into them. He was still there, and still feeling about as comfortable as a .22 cartridge in a 12 gauge gun, when the door closed behind her and he was left alone with his problems.

# ELEVEN

SHE TOOK LONGER than Turk had reckoned on and
he was pretty near fit to be tied when she got back.
The noise from downstairs had considerably
increased and she had to get a candle lit before she
would put the key in his hand. "Yeah," he said,
"that looks like it, all right."

"It is the one," she assured him. "I found out
where she was before I went down there after it.
We exchanged a few words. I thought it might be
wise to let her know what was planned; and it was
well that I did because that Kelly did not take any
chances. He went up and talked to her himself
before he would give me the key."

Turk gave it back to her and she said, "We will
have to move quickly. I think Kelly will send some
men to find and tell Bill."

"Yeah." Turk scowled. He hadn't thought of
this, either.

She pushed him toward the door. "There is a
large tree behind this place that has its feet in the
water. You bring the clothes and horses. She will
wait for you there."

"How you going to git her out of here?"

"She will have to go through this window—they have nailed the one in her room. But she has two blankets she will tear in half and with mine this should be enough. You'd better hurry."

Nick's place was doing a pretty fair business when Turk started down the stairs. Kelly had a helper back of the bar and four of the gambling rigs were surrounded. Thomas and Snow—the former facing the stairs—were gabbing with three other hard looking customers. Turk saw the hatchet-faced Thomas nudge Snow and mutter something to him out of the corner of his mouth. Snow looked up and snickered. Two of the others looked around.

Turk could feel his ears begin to burn. He was remembering that these wallopers had probably helped to make that boot sound when he'd been having his hoedown with Rita. But they didn't try to get in his way when he passed them. "How's tricks?" Kelly called, and Turk jerked a hand at him and shoved on through the batwings.

It was full dark outside and the wind had got up again. Turk, lengthening his stride, cut straight for the place where he had left his horse. He wasn't going to bother with no gooddam clothes. The sooner he and Holly got to whacking leather the better. He still felt mean about Bill but Holly's health and mental comfort were things he couldn't well ignore; and there was Rita, too, to be thought about. But he'd have to take care of first things first; and that Rita, from all he had seen of her, was pretty well able to take care of herself.

The boss wrangler was gone when Turk reached

the corral, but his handy man fetched out High Sailin. Turk threw his saddle on and hurriedly cinched up. He asked the fellow if he'd a nag he could borrow, something with bottom and a little burst of speed. "One of the boys just got in," Turk said, "and his mount's about done up."

The man shuffled off and came back with a brushscarred buckskin. "This yere bayo coyote oughta make it," he said, and Turk looked him over. The horse was built like a jackrabbit but Turk had forked enough good ones to grunt quick approval. He was scared to ask the man for a saddle. He'd put Holly on High Sailin.

Turk swung up and the man passed him the buckskin's halter shank. "Bound for Skeleton, are you?"

Turk looked down into the man's homely face. "A loose tongue has took care of more damn fools than shovels."

The fellow showed a sour grin. "You must be a new broom." Then he said, leaning nearer, "There's jest one thing you got to watch in this camp and that's to make almighty certain you don't cross up Curly Bill."

Turk circled in the dark and fetched his horses down off the mesa. He found it hard to restrain his impatience when he thought of Holly holed-up beside that tree and probably scared half out of her senses. He wasn't feeling too good himself with this business and was considerably plagued by recollections of Rita. When Bill heard about that key he sure as hell wasn't going to like it. Turk got to thinking he had been pretty all-fired thoughtless roping the kid into setting this deal up, then riding off and leaving her to weather Bill's wrath. Made him look like a stinker. Made him feel like one, too. He was half of a mind to ride back up there and get her.

He sat scowling a moment before he put High Sailin up the bed of the creek, hauling the buckskin by the halter shank behind him. The girl had done a lot for him but, damn it, a man had to tackle first things first and his obligation was unquestionably to Holly. If he hadn't taken advantage of her that day at the Willow Springs linecamp . . .

It was blacker down here than the inside of a cat, and the few stars he could see through the slat and flap of the sycamores didn't help no more than pouring water on a drowned rat. He had to leave the footing entirely up to the horses. Once a branch slapped him so hard across the face he came within a hair of going right plumb out of the saddle.

After that he kept an arm held up in front of him. But he couldn't shore off his uncomfortable thoughts about Rita or take away one jot of his uneasiness about Bill.

They'd be bound to come after him.

It wasn't the prospect of violence which had Turk sweating. He didn't believe Bill would take a gun to him. It was what Bill would think, him doing this to Bill after he'd taken Turk in like he had and made a place for him. They'd been friends, the way Turk saw it—good friends; and that was the way Turk wanted to stay with Bill, knowing all the while that they could never go

128

back to how things had been before Bill's bunch had grabbed Holly.

The creek's righthand bank became the side of the mesa, and every clack of a hoof against stone ran Turk's hackles up. His nerves became pulled so tight the whole back of his neck ached; and abruptly, black and ugly atop the treacherous slope, he saw the back of Nick's place against the lesser black of sky. It had a secretive sinister look crouched up there with the shine of yellow light filtering down through the trees' swaying branches.

He pulled up High Sailin to take a quick squint around, not locating anything but not feeling right either. The shadows up under those wind-bent branches looked thicker than smoke and were piled deep enough to have hidden away Geronimo and half his damned Apaches.

Turk didn't like it and High Sailin didn't either, nor the buckskin that came up now and stopped by his shoulder. The buckskin blew through his nose and High Sailin gingerly hunched himself as though quite ready to bolt if he got he least encouragement.

And suddenly both horses' ears pricked toward the blackness off to the left of Turk. After staring a moment Turk saw it too, a solid black in the wind-slapped shadows that couldn't be anything but a human shape. It was fright, not guts, that kept Turk from yanking the gun from his holster.

How long they stayed motionless staring at each other there was no way of telling, but abruptly Turk's pistol was in his grip, stiffly pointed. He had the hammer thumbed back but was afriad to let go of it lest the roar of the explosion bring the whole camp down on him.

When he got enough spit gathered to pull the words from his throat, he gruffed, "You, over there—come out of that!"

For long moments nothing happened, then the blackness stirred again and the darker chunk moved up to where he could see its arms were up even with its head; but that was about all the could see. But now a shift in the wind put a silver of light through the tossed-about branches and sweat came out and lay cold on Turk's cheekbones. The light only cut that shape across the middle but it showed him the remembered color of Holly's dress and the tails of her scarf hanging down from covering her hair up. He got the shakes so bad he nearly forgot to pouch his pistol.

The impatient shake of High Sailin's head brought him back to the pressure of passing time. "Don't stand there!" he growled, and came out of the saddle, exasperated with her. "Here—" he said, holding the reins out, "climb onto this horse and let's git the hell out of here!"

As she came forward through the gloom to take the reins from his grip, something in the way she moved caught at him and he went cold all over. And it wasn't just the water from the creek sucking down his boot tops.

His arm shot out and jerked the scarf off her hair and got hold of the front of her, pulling her toward him through the sliver of light. One look at that mop of black hair was aplenty.

"So you reckoned I'd go with you, never knowin'

the difference!" Choking with rage he snarled thickly: "Where is she?"

He saw the upsweep of her chin, her defiance; saw the curl of her lips. But when he started to yank the reins from her she cried, "Wait—I will tell you!" and grinned at him bleakly. "She is there where I found her—"

"And how did you git to be wearin' her things?"

"I said it was your wish—a part of the plan— that we should change. And because she is a fool she took them off and gave them to me. But I did not give her mine." She shook the hair back off her cheeks and laughed openly. "She waits in the room with no clothes for you to save her."

"You damn hellcat!" Turk swore, coming within an inch of striking her. "Give me the key!"

Her grin turned cruel, mocking him. "The key I have left in the door—on the outside," and she laughed again as he flung into the saddle. "It is too late for you to save her. Curly Bill was on the stairs when I came down from the window on the rope we made with her blankets."

# TWELVE

TURK HAD NO clear remembrance of how he got up that slope from the creek. Reaction was still churning violently through him when he sprang down from the saddle in front of Nick's batwings. He tried to tear from his mind its seething load of frustration and anger that he might, at least with some degree of clarity, assess the damage her prank had done; but his thoughts were too wild, his confusion too great for reasoning. He knew only that he must reach Holly at once.

He shoved Nick's slatted doors off his elbows and rushed in with a hand flying back for his gun. The fetid air with its reek of unwashed bodies, bad breath, smoke and whisky, almost gagged him; the glare of the lamps half blinded him and noise rolled against him in a solid wall of sound.

The place was packed.

The day shift from Galey's smelter crammed the gambling rigs and bar six deep. Horse-soldiers in blue tunics set off by yellow neck rags, whiskered desert rats and redshirted miners showed thinly sandwiched in with these, rubbing shoulders with

132

big-hatted cowhands and dark-faced vaqueros from below the international line. Turk had no heed for any of this. His stare, cutting over the smoky sea of shifting headgear, was riveted on the spindle-railed balcony as he bitterly fought to get through the sweating crush.

"Watch where you're goin'—"

"Get out of my way!"

"Who the hell you shovin'!"

He was trapped in the solid middle of it, furious, when he saw Holly's door opening and her coming out of it and Bill right back of her, talking and laughing, with a hand on her shoulder. She had on a blue shirt like the one Turk was wearing and pants, just like a man, with their bottoms thrust into fancy-topped boots that must have set someone back more than a little.

It was the pants Turk's shocked stare clung to longest. And it wasn't just he way she filled them out that got him either, though it may have had something to do with the dark rush of blood that pounded into his cheeks. Decent women didn't wear pants!

With her thighs pressed against the balcony's rail she stood with Bill, staring over the packed room. She moved her hands and her mouth moved and Turk saw Bill chuckle, and her grinning back at him.

Turk couldn't understand it. But that was Holly, all right. No mistake about that part.

He saw Bill taking a squint at his timepiece, turning it around so that she could eye it too. Turk saw her lips move again and Bill throwing back his head in a laugh. Bill patted her shoulder. They were turning away then and Bill, leaning closer, was handing her something which to Turk's incredulous eyes looked almighty like a key. While his tangled emotions were still reeling under this he saw her turn at the door, lifting a smiling face which Bill, pulling her against him, kissed with bold assurance.

Turk swung around, blindly making for the bat-wings. He ran squarely into a man and shoved him aside without even looking. "Better hev a drink," came Willbrandt's voice somewhere to the left of him—"you sure look like you could use one." Turk caught a whiff of the man's peppermint breath but brushed on past him without a word. He knocked somebody else out of his way and kept going.

He was less than ten feet from the half-leaf doors when they squeaked and swung inward and there was Rita in Holly's dress staring impudently at him. He didn't stop to think but caught her roughly by the arm. "Come on—let's git out of this goddamn camp!"

Thomas came through the doors with Charlie Snow on his heels and, seeing Turk and the girl, pulled up directly in their path. The wedge-faced Thomas, too drunk to grasp Turk's condition, gave Snow a nudge that promised some fun and had his mouth halfway open when Turk hit him in the stomach. As the man came jackknifing forward, eyes bulging, Turk hung one on his chin and Thomas went down and out in one motion.

Snow's hand started hipward. Something glimpsed in Turk's stare stopped the hand short of leather. A whisper of escaping breath leaked out

134

of him and he backed carefully off till he was out of Turk's way.

"Hey Red—Turkey Red!" came Bill's bull-throated shout; and before Turk could move Bill was up with him, laughing and slapping Turk's shoulder.

And Turk stood there, tongue tied, with his face like pounded metal, listening to the boom of Bill's jovial voice and suddenly inexplicably, hating it. Hating the feel of Bill's hand on his shoulder and seeing a heap of things now which anyone, he reckoned, but a damnfool kid would have savvied from the start and had the sense to sheer away from.

"Time to be hittin' leather," Bill rumbled, stepping between Turk and Rita with that easy assurance Turk had recently so admired, and with his hand on Turk's shoulder slipping Turk on through the batwings. The blackness of the windy street came up and closed like fog around them and Bill, twisting his head, wanted to know where Jake and Ringo were, and Snow's reedy tones said they were over in back of Jack Dahl's place waiting with the Clantons and the horses.

Turk caught up High Sailin's reins and, twisting away from Bill's hand, swung into the saddle. Stilwell and Willbrandt got hold of their broncs and mounted too. And Turk, wanting out of this, knew he couldn't get out; that he was sucked up into this now with the rest of them, chained and shackled by knowledge that wouldn't ever let him go. He was part of Bill's border legion now and a man didn't quit Bill Graham and stay healthy.

Skeleton Canyon was a runway of smugglers that curled like a snake through the wildest regions of the Peloncillo Mountains, entering them from the Animas Valley and coming out near Douglas at the far southern end of the San Simon.

Noon's sun filled its trough with a blinding glare that had every inch of Turk crying for water. His eyes felt like baked marbles in the trapped heat crawling off the smoking rocks, and there was no talk now and, among the others, no smoking on Bill's orders. He had hidden them well, leaving Turk and himself wholly alone on the trail.

They were here to latch onto a mule train which, according to Old Man Clanton, had come up out of Mexico to pick up guns and bullets in Tucson where the fat little merchants were salting away a tidy profit from such strictly cash transactions. Even in the light of his own new and private views about Bill, Turk couldn't find much fault with laying a trap to stop and rob a gang of Mexican smugglers.

Still, he didn't like it. Nor did he care for Bill's reticence with regard to that business of the key and Holly's clothes. Nor the odd way Bill, every once in a while, would look at him. Since Bill wasn't one to hide his anger it seemed obvious Holly hadn't mentioned Turk's name. But the barkeep would certainly have told him about the key and Holly would have named Rita on account of the clothes and to explain her own lack of them. Was Bill then so pleased with the results he'd forgiven Rita? Or had she been dealt with after they'd left? Turk felt sick every time he considered this and was so worked up he didn't half know what he was doing.

A couple of carpenter birds began berating each other over in the willows that fringed the gurgling creek, and a road runner squawked and whacked his bill against the shale and kind of teetered on his legs as though about to collapse. Suddenly he went bounding straight up into the air and came down with a sparrow in his mouth and started running.

Turk wished he had a drink, and wasn't thinking of the kind he could have by going to the creek. He wished those Mexicans would hurry up and get here. The plan, as he'd heard Bill tell it, didn't call for any shooting. Bill and Turk were to handle the stopping, holding the dons in talk while Bill looked them over and gave the rest of his outfit time to get set for any last minute changes which might seem desirable. Once Bill was sure they'd got hold of the right party he was to whistle a snatch from *La Paloma*, after which he and Turk would move on up the canyon—this to block escape in case the dons attempted to bolt.

The place picked to get the jump on these smugglers was known as the Devil's Kitchen and, considering the heat, Turk thought it aptly named.

There was a kind of greasy shine to Bill's face as he lounged in the saddle, sleepy looking as his horse. He could have passed, like Jake Gauze, for a Mexican; it was, in fact, what he proposed to do.

A week ago Turk would have felt greatly complimented to have been teamed off with Bill in this fashion. Now, with more understanding, he sourly suspected he'd been chosen to work this part of the deal in the hope his looks would set at rest any feelings of disquiet their appearance might cause in the minds of the intended victims. He was more than half convinced here was the reason—and the only one—Bill had taken him on in the first place.

He felt a strong distaste for the entire venture. The way he looked at it, robbing Mexicans was in the same class with taking candy from a kid. No tricks needed. Davy Crockett had told it all when he said one toothless old half-awake Texican could hold off thirty of the best the dons could manage with one paw tied and both legs broke. Turk was a heap more concerned with his uncomfortable thoughts of Rita when, faint through the sunlit silence, came the far-off up-canyon tinkle of a bell.

Bill came out of his slouch. He rasped the back of his hand across his jowls and yawned and stretched. Then he looked over at Turk. "I'll do the talkin'. If them dons happens to come up with any fancy notions, you foller my lead. Don't try anything on your own hook."

Not till Turk nodded did Bill remove his gaze. Then he took a look at his pistols and, putting them away, bent a keen inspecting frown across the skylined rocks and chaparral masking the top of the nearest rim. Evidently satisfied, he kneed his pony out into the trail.

By this time the bells were considerably closer. Dingle dangle, creaking of leather, plopping hoofs and a mumble of voice sounds made quite a commotion kicked around through the rocks and shored up with echoes. One of the bunch was even tickling a guitar, as though smuggling was no different than punching cows or any other job. Mexicans, Turk concluded, didn't have sense enough to pound sand down a rat hole.

And there they came, strung out all over, with a bighatted don on a prancing black stallion at the head of them—the *patron*, like enough, to judge by his trappings. There was another fellow riding just a couple of strides behind him; this, Turk reckoned, was probably the boss the don hired to pass orders to the rest of them. He had a corn husk cigarette stuck in his face. And, back of this pair, came the mules picking their feet up to the musical clink clank of bulging pack saddles— *aparejos*, the Mexes called them.

Turk could see the mules in a long weaving line curling around through the rocks and the dust they were raising. He counted eight additional riders, at least three of them looking to be younger than he was; it was the handsomest of these that was playing the guitar. He had tiny golden bells on his sombrero. The *patron* had, too.

He looked a bit taken aback at finding Turk and Bill in front of him and sent a gabble of Spanish flying over his shoulder that, when relayed by the second man, brought the whole train to a standstill. The pretty kid quit fooling with his guitar and the cigarette-smoking *segundo* put a hand to his gun stock. The whole bunch looked worried and Turk could see they weren't fighters.

Bill, stopping his horse, grinned and spoke politely, describing himself as a local rancher out with one of his cowboys trying to find some strayed cattle. He cussed the July heat and inquired about the old fellow's health in the don's own lingo, quite as though he considered Mexicans the salt of the earth.

He made quite an impression. The old don smiled and quit chewing his lip. He said he was Miguel Garcia of Hermosillo, and asked about Bill's health. Bill allowed he was still able to totter around, and after swapping a few more pleasantries Don Miguel described himself as a merchant of pots and pans bound for Tucson to trade for Navajo blankets. He said friends had told him these mountains were filled with robbers and, while he had no money, he had been forced to mortgage his store to secure this load of kitchenware and would be ruined if thieves should take it.

Bill said his cook might find use for a few pans if the price was right. The old don looked shocked. His poor stuff, he explained, was much too crude for so grand a *caballero;* as the Virgin well knew, the cheapest he could find, fit only for paupers and Indians. He said, crossing himself, he hoped he would not encounter any bandits.

"With pots and pans?" Bill laughed. "The only real outlaws around these parts are too busy stealing cows to bother with anything else." He said, still speaking Spanish, "Now if it was gold your packs were filled with, or a bunch of those silver dollars, you might have something to get in a sweat about."

Bill winked, whacking his high when he said this, as though making up something to laugh at. The old don's grin looked a bit on the parched side and the pockmarked *segundo,* spitting out his cigarette, dropped a hand to his gun again.

Bill made out not to notice. "Well, so long," he said, and picked up his reins. Don Miguel said, "Go with God," and waved a hand. The Mexicans with the mules got back in their saddles and prodded the train into movement. All the bells started tinkling, hoofs plopped, leather squeaked and the bulging *aparejos* clinked and clanked.

Turk saw Bill swivel a furtive glance at the rim. Turk followed him down the line, listening to Bill tossing quips at the mule men about the fun they would have with the girls at Tucson and how long it would take to count the skirts they had on them and which would be the first to cry hello at what these guarded. Turk had heard the like more times than he could remember but he thought it a cruel jest with Bill figuring to grab all their silver.

When they reached the young fellow with the guitar, Bill said, "Can you play *La Paloma?*"

"But, of course, senor," he assured Bill, smiling.

"Go ahead," Bill said—"there's a buck in it for you," and the kid right away started plunking and chuckling while Bill joined his whistle to the lilt of its chorus. "Something else?" the kid asked when he'd finished. "No," Bill grinned, "that ought to do the first rate," and flipped him the promised cartwheel.

The dust was thick back here at the end of the train but Turk could see the pleased look on the kid's face as he caught it. "*Mil* gracias!" he cried, sweeping off his belled hat. "May the saints—"

That was far as he got. The rest was lost in a racket of rifles. Gouts of flame lividly lanced from the brush and rocks of the canyon wall. Anguished cries and frantic curses mingled thinly with the piercing screams of terrified horses and the frightened braying of the panicked mules. In that first unbelieving glance Turk saw three of the Mexicans reel out of their saddles while a fourth, with foot hung in stirrup, was dragged bouncing away through a curtain of dust.

"Git that old geezer with them bells on his bonnet!"

"Git 'em all!" Bill yelled—"every sonofabitch' one of 'em!"

Turk stared at the man with a crawling horror, remembering with bitter clarity how this same Curly Bill, not an hour gone by, had declared when Turk brought up the matter there would be no need for shooting.

Turk yelled at Bill, his face mottled with shame and fury as he drove High Sailin through a tangle of motion, trying to catch hold of Bill's arm. "Are you crazy, man? God damn it, you said—"

The guitar kid with the grin still froze to his face badly reeled in the saddle but clutched a grip in the mane of his horse and stayed on. Bill's swiveling guns tumbled a man from his mount so close to the boy the blood spattered on him and the kid, with a squawk, clapped heels to his horse and took off in wild flight with his yell sailing back like it was made out of goose quills.

"Git that kid!" Bill snarled, savagely triggering on empties.

With leaves and twigs raining down across its rump the kid's bronc tore through the screen of willows bordering the creek. Bill sheathed one smoking emptied gun and was fumbling fresh loads from his belt to the other, while attempting to drive his pitching horse after the kid, when the pockmarked *segundo* came tearing up out of the dust with a blazing rifle, driving straight at Bill.

Turk fired without thought and saw the smuggler's horse plow head first through the shale. Flung clear, the lanky Mexican scrambled to his feet and lunged at Bill with a lifted knife. There was no time for nice distinctions. Bill, Turk knew. The Mexican was a stranger. Turk shot the Mexican through the head.

Bill was down, too, but now he rolled to his knees. He came onto his feet and picked up his pistols, shaking the sand out, replacing spent cartridges with loads from his belt. He looked around and found his hat. He cuffed the worst of the dust out and clapped it on. He glared around at Turk then with that shock of black hair curling down across his forehead. The both of them knew Turk had ruined his aim but he didn't say anything. He swung around on his heel and went clanking his spurs toward where the rest of his bunch was coming down off the rim.

The jamboree was over. Two mules had been killed and lay with bursted packs where the guns had dropped them. Dead Mexicans were everywhere and one of them, not so dead, tried to drag himself up with a whimpering groan. Jake Gauze, spying the man, emptied a pistol into him and then, stepping closer, crashed a boot into his face.

Reaction hit Turk then and he rode into the willows, retching. Ringo was cursing the vanished mules which had stampeded downcanyon in the wake of what horses had got clear of the slaughter. Even through his misery Turk could hear the vicious swearing and the angry bickering of Billy Clanton and two of the others rolling the stiffs for rings and cash.

Turk hung over the saddle with both hands choking the apple till nothing more would come up. Spent and weak he got down then, shivering and sweating, and staggered over to the water. He flopped on his belly and closed both eyes, shuddering. He put his face in the murmurous creek but couldn't wash away the taste. Nor was he able to drown the screams or drive from recoiling memory the hideous sights he'd been forced to witness. He guessed these things must be a part of him forever and in an access of horror he wished that he could die.

But the worst of it finally passed and he got shakily to his feet. His mind shied away from thoughts of Bill. He tried to twist himself a smoke but after tearing three papers he put the rest of the stuff in his pockets. And that was when he saw Gauze watching him.

The black browed squatty toad of a man stood grinning in the willows. Anger came into Turk's throat like bile and all the frustrated bitterness of these last weeks threatened to fling his hand to gun butt when Jake laughed at him with open jeering mockery. But this was what Gauze wanted, it was a baleful shine in his hooded stare, in the curl of the fist hanging spraddled above the man's cutaway hoster.

And suddenly Turk was cool again, master of himself with a strange new certainty that never had flowed through his veins before. He saw a puzzled light creep through the gleam of Jake's stare and turned away from the man, stepping into his saddle.

Jake cursed him with all the foul oaths of the border and Turk's ears turned red but he didn't let it throw him. In the grip of his new assurance he could hear the man's foulness without letting it push him one inch from his decision.

"Rabbit," Jake growled with his lips curled back, scornful. "Not even a jack—jest a runty damn weavily cottontail!" He scrinched his mouth up and spat. "All right, Diapers. Come along. The boss has got somethin' he's cravin' to say to you."

He wheeled off through the brush and Turk let High Sailin follow. When they came out on the trail Bill was putting Ringo in charge of going after the mules which by now were probably scattered halfway to Douglas. He looked up and around with his eyes like hot iron when they came slamming into Turk's; then he took a second look and semed to control himself with an effort.

He got onto his horse, which one of the others had fetched up, and sat awhile scowling before impatience swung his shoulders about to wave Ringo off with the most of the rest of them on their hunt for the mule packs. Only three men stayed with him—Willbrandt, Gauze and that whiskered Jim Hughes.

Bill brought his look back to Turk.

"Reckon you saved my hide," he said, trying to call up his grin and making pretty rough work of it, "so we'll fergit a few things that ain't been settin' too good with me." That was how he put it though his eyes didn't look like they were about to forget anything. Then he said with the growl

145

getting into his voice again, "Just keep in mind hereafter that when I give an order every guy in this outfit jumps! You understand?"

"Nothin' wrong with my hearin'."

"You better remember it, too."

Turk didn't answer. It was Bill that turned away.

The others, with wooden faces, made a business of climbing into their saddles—all but Jake. Jake rubbed the flats of his pantlegs and hunched his bowed shoulders, looking from Bill to Turk and back again. At last, with a sneer, he got onto his horse.

"I'm headin' for town," Turk said; and Bill's roan cheeks came around with his eyes, bright and narrow, looking almost like glass.

"I'm goin' now," Turk added, and put High Sailin crossways of the trail.

A vicious anticipation leaped into Jake's stare. Jim Hughes' whiskered cheeks stayed neutral. Bill's eyes became pieces of jet in his dark face and the peppermint snapped between Willbrandt's teeth.

"Hell," Bill said with a queer strangled gruffness, "we're all goin' now—"

Turk didn't wait for them. He didn't crowd High Sailin but kept him out in front like he was mindful to ride by himself. Jake's hand slid to gun stock but Bill caught his wrist and let Turk get away with it.

"Not yet," he growled. "I still got use fer that fool."

# THIRTEEN

It was dark when they came by a short cut to Galeyville, dark and close to midnight—not that this made any great amount of difference. Curly Bill's new headquarters was an all-night camp and Turk caught the unholy din of it long before High Sailin's tired hoofs brought them up onto the mesa. Lamps in the saloons and honkytonks stippled the gray dust of the street in a patchwork of light and shadow and the wail of the fiddles cut above the locust sound of men's voices. Six Key Joe, at the piano in Nick's bar, was making the ivories talk.

Turk was passing Jack McConaghey's saloon when he stared back over his shoulder to gauge how much time he might have to find Rita. It was impossible to tell. He couldn't see Bill or the three who were with BIll, but it was a foregone conclusion they were not far behind—a quarter mile perhaps.

Turk knew he was in for trouble but he wasn't expecting the kind that came at him. He was turning High Sailin to make for Nick's tierack, with the light from McConaghey's splashing full on him, when a shape shoved out of the mouth of an alley. "Hold up there!" this man called; and Turk—lips pulling tight across the shine of his teeth—recognized the voice of Buck Linderstrom.

He saw the lift of gun steel in the Roman 4 man's fist. And at the same time, off to the left of him, another crouched shape came out of the shadows. "*Where is she?*" Ruebusch's voice snarled.

"Now wait a minute—" Turk said, and dived from the saddle under the scream of lead as gunflame ripped the blackness to the right of him. He struck the dust rolling, letting the horse go, and came up breathing hard with his gun clearing leather. A shape darted across the light from McConaghey's and he put two shots into that bedlam of sound. He heard a man screech and saw Strehl going around in a staggering circle.

Something cuffed at Turk's waist and his straining eyes picked up Linderstrom as High Sailin veered off with head down and heels flying. The man was almost on top of him when Turk whipped his gun up, the two pistols roaring almost in unison. The range boss grabbed at his stomach and collapsed. The man on Turk's right started throwing lead at him.

Something hit him like a fist, smashing Turk half around; and he heard men yelling and, above this, the rushing pound of fast traveling hoofs. He got onto one knee in the strangling dust and saw Ruebusch, against the lights, running toward him, and he hollered at the man but Ruebusch kept coming.

Turk clawed himself upright and hoof sounds

hammered the fronts of the buildings. He wanted to live. He knew he ought to cut Ruebusch down but he couldn't do it. He saw Bill's face and Jake's above the manes of their horses and he tried to warn Ruebusch, crazily holding his fire with the bullets slapping round him, pleading with the man and finally, furiously, cursing him. The sudden crash of Winchesters threw up a roaring wall of sound. The man's legs went out from under him, spilling him all spreaddled out into the ballooning dust of the street.

Incredibly he got up again, stumbling toward Turk, still trying to kill him, the hammer of his gun over and over striking futilely against the heads of emptied shells. Once more Jake's rifle crashed. Turk saw Ruebusch's hat fall off. The man stopped moving and rose, straightening fully, on the toes of his boots. The gun fell out of his hand. He took one additional step and crumpled.

The wind had fallen. A brooding silence closed around Turk, broken only by the scamper of fingers across the keys of the piano in Babcock's bar.

Turk felt the weight of the pistol he was holding. The gun sagged to his side and his knees started shaking. It was reaction, he knew. The horror came and then, hard on top of it, Bill's call.

In an access of revulsion Turk struck out for Nick's blindly. He didn't want to have to listen to Bill, didn't want even to have to look at him again. Bile came into the brassy taste of his throat. He heard the ring of spurred boots as someone behind him broke into a lumbering run. Turk didn't look. He didn't wait, either.

149

He pushed through Nick's batwings and the warmth of the place and its smell came at him through the wavering sway of that sea of white faces. He thought he was going to be sick.

He fought the nausea down and men opened up a path for him the way, he suddenly remembered, they had always done for Bill. This too had been one of the things he had coveted; the right of fame, he thought, hating it.

He reached the stairs and started up them, hearing the batwings squeak behind him. He could feel the drag of men's stares reaching after him and his feet purely seemed like they were weighted with stove lids. He put a hand on the banister to steady himself. In this frozen hush his boots made an intolerable racket on the steps.

His head came level with the top of them. There was something going on beyond the red-yellow shine of Rita's shut door; he caught the wheeze of labored breathing, the sudden frantic rip of cloth.

If the goddam stairs would only stay where they'd been built! Still gripping the banister he got to the top of them just as the door of Rita's room was yanked open. He saw the scratched and sweat-filmed gleam of Thomas' face and lunged for him. But his legs were unwieldy and his feet wouldn't track right. Thomas, ducking, twisted away from him and spun onto the balcony, dragging at his gun.

Turk spun, too, reeling after him. The forgotten pistol in his fist laid open Thomas' white face from left temple to chin. The man staggered backward and with a screech went through the rail. Turk, off balance, would have gone through after him if Rita hadn't grabbed him.

He shook his head to clear his eyes and thought it was time Kelly got the lamps lit. Under his left ribs the shirt was sticking to him soddenly and Rita was crying something over and over and through the deepening gloom he saw Jake's face with Curly Bill's behind it; and he said, "I'm takin' her out of this!"

And Jake Gauze said, "You ain't goin' noplace—" and that was all Turk heard. The blackness was complete.

For a long and miserable while about the only thing Turk was conscious of was the feel of a cool comforting hand softly pushing the sweaty hair off his forehead. Later, other fancies came occasionally to wander through the jumbled impressions of his fevered delirium. This was generally in the mornings when he'd be staring up into those outside trees watching the way the wind shook their tops, wishing Holly's cool hands would come back to him; and, sometimes, in the darkness he would put out an arm and, finding her, pull her closer, hearing the troubled whisper of her voice but not understanding what it was she seemed trying to tell him. The best times, though, were when he'd find her lips with his and feel hers come back at him, desperately almost.

Those times he'd tell her things he wouldn't have told another soul, and he would feel the sobs shaking her and couldn't understand why she'd be crying now about it when she hadn't cried at Willow Springs. He guessed he never would savvy women. But as soon as he got things straightened with Bill they'd go off someplace by themselves, he'd tell her, and build a spread of their own where folks didn't know anything about her or him. And she would kiss him, queer like, and sometimes she'd cry, not making no sound but hanging hold of him like she would never let go. Once she said, "*Si*—yes, yes," like she was dying— "*si, querido*, love of my soul," and it would give him a laugh—a real belly laugh—to think of her talking like a dadburned Mex. "Sleep," she said. "Pretty soon you will be strong and perhaps get drunk, forgetting these beautiful plans we have made. Perhaps you will curse me and these nights you have spent here," and she'd got up and hurried out.

Sometimes Turk couldn't figure her at all.

And then he was on the mend again. At first just sitting up in bed with pillows back of him, afterwards graduating to a chair. It was a red-letter day when he got onto the porch. He decided this shack was quite a ways from town. He didn't hear much of its racket except such times as he would wake up at night. There was a grove of live oak about this hideaway of his, and the different green of juniper. The only person he saw was the old Mexican woman who came each day to clean the house and take care of him. During this convalescence his thoughts only touched Holly once and then with a scorn mainly directed at himself. He didn't recall the hallucinations of his fever.

It was on the morning of the third day prior to sitting up that he first saw the old woman. She told him her name was Dolores. He was still pretty weak but his head was clear. He asked her how long he had been in the bed. "Ten days," she said, counting her fingers.

He guessed it had been touch and go for a while. He must have lost a lot of blood.

The first day he sat up he asked about his horses. The old woman said they were being cared for in town. "Why not here?" Turk wanted to know. He had his own guess at the answer but he didn't find out from Dolores.

Five days later she let him walk under the trees, but he soon tired and was glad to get back to his chair on the porch. He must have been a lot closer to not making it than he'd figured.

When she called him in to a kind of mulligan she made that was better than it looked, he asked her bluntly why Rita was so pointedly staying away from him. The old woman shrugged. "Has she gone?" Turk demanded—"has she left town?"

Rita, she said, was dancing at Babcock's.

He didn't know what had made him think old Dolores would know the girl. He was sure now it was Rita who employed her. "And does she never ask of me?"

"Every night," the woman chuckled. "She gives me the medicine to put on that place in your side."

Turk had reckoned as much, remembering how she had cared for him at Charleston. He kept his voice casual. "How long was she out here before you showed up?"

The old woman grinned and shook her head at him.

"Well," Turk said testily, "How'd she git me out here?"

"Curly Bill help her. And Pancho Stealwell. That

Jake Gauze no like it. Say pretty soon kill you."
She drew a finger across her throat. "Curly Bill
laugh."

Turk got up and buckled his shell belt around
him and spent the next hour cleaning and oiling
his pistol. Then he dumped out the loads and
replaced them with cartridges from the unopened
box that was still in his coat pocket. It had been
Bill, like enough, who had given out the order to
keep his horses in town. Turk had seen too much
to be allowed to pull out.

With his morose thoughts again on Rita, Turk's
mind cast back through the hours he had lain in
that bed watching the tops of wind-bent trees; and
he unearthed a few hazy recollections that
darkened and tightened the twist of his scowl. Of
course. No wonder she was staying away from him
now. In the blind alleys of his delirium he had
probably called her "Holly." He seemed to remember that she had cried a lot . . .

When Dolores got ready to leave that evening he
fished in his pocket and gave her a handful of
coins and told her to bring him a razor.

She was back with one the following morning. It
must have been used to shave hogs. He spent a
couple of hours getting the blade in shape before
he dared put it against his skin. Even then he
looked like he'd been pulled through a knothole.
When he finally got done he cornered Dolores in
the midst of her cooking. "What's the latest gossip
flyin' around?" he wanted to know.

She said Johnny Behan had got the sheriff's
star. "Guess who he has made deputy—Pancho
Stealwell!"

It did seem a little raw, Turk thought, to go pinning a badge on Frank Stilwell's shirt. All past favors apppreciated, it still looked pretty brazen. It had been said, and with considerable justice, Frank had worked the roads so much in these parts all the stage teams stopped whenever they got within sound of his voice. The way it looked to Turk this country was getting so all-fired crooked a man couldn't half the time tell up from down.

"What about Bill?"

She said that, according to what she'd heard, Bill and some of the others had gone down into Sonora right after they'd got back from Skeleton Canyon and run off a big herd of steers to Clanton's ranch in the Las Animas. Clanton was to locate a market. While Bill and his gang were waiting for the Clantons to get another herd together, a bunch of Mexican cowboys, trailing over from Sonora, had caught the bunch napping and recovered their stock. Bill, Ringo, Gauze and some more of them had gone after and caught them in San Luis Pass. They'd been a whale of a fight. Fourteen Mexicans had been killed and Bill's crowd had headed back for Clanton's with the steers. On the way they had tortured like Apaches the eight wounded vaqueros they had rounded up after the battle.

Turk left the shack. He had seen enough during that mule train deal to realize this report was in keeping with the real character of Bill's outfit as he had now come to know it. These were not cowboys. They were renegades, wolves of the chaparral, vicious conscienceless killers no more burdened by scruples than a pack of mad dogs.

155

It had not been easy for him to arrive at this estimate; and the possibilities it turned loose in his mind were too infinite, to harassing for Turk to sit around with. He quit the shack knowing he had to face these things.

He'd no idea how long he prowled or where that distracted jaunt had taken him. But it was a man who came back, a man tired and peaked but one who had taken account of himself and found where he stood in relation to his fellows.

He had been pretty foolish.

Another week crawled past, seven days of dread and worry. On the eighth he cleaned his gun again and in the middle of the morning set out for town.

Harassed as he had been Turk had wasted no time in idleness. He'd devoted most of those hours to regaining his strength and making himself fit by many miles of tramping through the dappled sun and shadow underneath the live oaks. He had worn dusty paths through the sparse grass and prickly pear and had done much practising beneath the trees with his pistol. Never, firing a shot, but whirling and twisting like a man with the twitches, yanking his gun from leather from ever conceivable type of disadvantage. He wasn't satisfied yet but the pressure of time and of his hunger for Rita wouldn't let him put off longer coming to grips with this thing.

The first problem, of course, was to get hold of his horses. He went straight to the corral from which he'd borrowed the buckskin the night his plan to free Holly had fizzled. Neither animal was in sight.

Turk didn't waste any words. He told the old wrangler he was looking for his horses. The man looked at him without any particular expression. "Thought you was borryin' that dun fer someone else."

"I was. And still am."

"Well, you ain't borryin' him here."

"You know where he's at?"

"Don't know an' don't wanta know." The old man, tightening his jaws about his cud, turned away.

Turk caught hold of his arm. "This is important—"

The old fellow jerked loose. He scrinched his lips and spat. "You'll get nothin' outa me. You won't get outa this camp, neither."

Turk looked at him narrowly. "Why won't I git out?"

"Because Bill's done passed the orders."

"You mean he's having me watched?"

"I dunno about that. But you won't get no horse, an' you better not try to make off with any. I warned you not to go crossin' up Bill!"

Turk, turning away, went on up the street. This was going to be even less easy than he'd figured. But he could measure the problem now with a cool and uncomplicated interest. Bill had thrown down the gauntlet when he put Turk afoot. The past was canceled out. There was no strings on Turk now. He had no further need for guessing. From here on out it was going to be toe-to-toe slugging with hell's doors open and yawning.

Turk crossed over to Nick Babcock's. Curly Bill wasn't under the trees with his beer; his horse wasn't at the tie rail.

Turk was just as well pleased. He wasn't nursing any illusions about the outcome if he were forced to cross guns with Bill. He pushed through Nick's batwings, hanging fire by the wall until his eyes could make out who was in this gray gloom.

Three men were at the bar. There was nobody at the tables.

"Well," Kelly said, "you finally made it, did you?"

The three heads came around. Charlie Snow, Jim Hughes and Tex Willbrandt. The memory of something tugged the corners of Snow's mouth. Tex, cold sober and with the inevitable peppermint lozenge padding out one cheek, called, "H'are you, feller!" and beckoned him over.

Turk shook his head and lifted one of the chairs off the top of a table. Tex came over with his glass and his eyes didn't miss much. "Still feelin' pretty puny, eh?"

"I've felt better," Turk said grimly. "What's the chances of you roundin' up a couple of horses?"

"Damn poor." Lowering his voice with a covert look toward the bar, Tex said, "I tried to tell you once what this outfit was like. You're stuck with it now. William's laid the law down. No horses for you or it will be too bad for somebody."

"What's the idea?"

"Well," Willbrandt mumbled, kind of chewing it over, "it looks like there's somethin' getting ready to come up where nobody in the bunch but mebbe you kin get the job done." He said to the question in Turk's eyes. "I think the boss is figurin' on sackin' Matamoros."

Turk half got up and then dropped back in his chair. He said grinning, "Quit hoorahin' me."

"I wish to Gawd I was," Tex growled. "This ain't no bull. He's just brash enough to try it. Told Jim Hughes they got statues in a church down there made outen solid silver. He's had me scoutin' wagons—"

"Wagons!" Turk looked at him dumbfounded. "They've got a garrison at Matamoros and at least two forts with cannons. He must be off his rocker!"

"You don't have to convince me," Tex sighed lugubriously. "He's up to somethin', all right. Won't let a one of us off the mesa. Only thing that's been holdin' him up is waitin' fer you to get well, I reckon."

He sloshed the whisky in his glass, morosely watching Hughes and Snow push away from the bar. Turk listened to them dragging their spurs toward the doors. He saw Tex glaring after Snow. "That ugly bastard's had it in fer you ever since you knocked his pardner off the balcony that night."

"Kill him?"

"It might better of. He won't never be the same again."

"Where's Rita?"

Willbrandt gave him a sharp look. "And that's another one'd sooner see you buried than not— that good fer nothin' brother of hers. If it wasn't fer Bill he'd of fixed you already."

"I don't even know the guy—"

"Hell you don't. You know Jake Gauze, don'tcha? That's who I'm talkin' about. He's said

159

flat out you're a spy Earp's planted on us and more'n a few of 'em believe it. Which is still another reason you better figure to stay put. Him and John Ringo swing a heap of weight in this outfit."

Turk scowled at his fist. He knew he had to try anyway, even if the whole camp came after him. Tex was watching him. Turk said, "There's no need for you to git mixed up in this. Just tell me where the horses are and—"

"Man, they'll blast you into doll rags!"

Turk said, "Where's Rita?"

"Up in her room, I guess. Sleepin'." The rusty-haired Willbrandt shook his head. "Hate to see you try it, kid. If you'd wait a spell . . ." He must have seen Turk's mind was made up. He swore irritably. "Your horse and that buckskin are over back of Jack Dahl's. Bill's keepin' a watch on 'em —Joe Hill and one of the Clanton's. I'll go—"

"You'll stay right here. If you've got to do somethin' you can tell Rita and Holly I'll meet them back of McCon—"

"You damn idjit," Tex growled, "you won't get ten feet—"

"All right," Turk said, pushing up from the table, I'll go tell them myself." But Willbrandt caught his arm, pulling him down again.

"By Gawd, you're crazier'n Bill. At least don't drag that doll-faced one into it. She's—"

"Tex," Turk broke in. "I rode for Ruebusch's outfit. It's on account of me he got killed. The least I can do is try to git his wife out of this." It was a moral obligation the way Turk looked at it. Holly might be selfish and shallow, and maybe a few other things he didn't want to think about, but she was at heart a good woman living a life that was worse than death. He hadn't forgotten what he'd seen on the balcony, but the way he saw it now she'd been acting a part with Bill, cozening the man till she could get away from him. She couldn't possibly care for . . .

"It'll be the first time," Tex grumbled, "I ever helped a man commit suicide, but if you're bound to do it I'll tell 'em. Back of McConaghey's. When do you want 'em there?"

"Give me half an hour," Turk said, discovering Kelly's stare fixed upon them. Kelly kind of jerked and swiped his rag along the bar with somewhat more vigor than looked to be called for. Turk watched him a moment, then got up and went out. He didn't reckon the barkeep could have heard enough to matter. He might, however, decide to tell Bill they'd been chinning.

Turk snorted the frown off his face and went on. Getting frittery as a nervous horse, he thought. Let the old fool tell Bill; by that time they'd be off this damned mesa. He hoped Tex wasn't going to get in trouble over this.

He sauntered all the way down to the far end of the street, trying to build up the notion he had nothing more important on his mind than his hat. He even shot the breeze a while with the barber, Ridge Cullum, who was squatting on his stoop mashing flies with a talcum box. Every time a new crop would bed down on this slaughter he would grind the box down again, smearing a few more into the bloody boards while he grumbled and cussed at the state of his business.

"Some days," he said, "there just ain't enough hours to take care of these sports, then I'll go for two weeks without splittin' a whisker. Times, by Gawd, is changin'! A lot of these bums is shavin' themselves and they'd sooner go dirty than wait for the tub. Used to be a feller'd get his hair cut every ten days, reg'lar as clock work. Now they wait till it's curlin' round their collars! Take a look at that shelf of tonics—that'll show you what this trade is a-comin' to. Ain't sold a drop for nigh onto six weeks!" He slammed the talcum box down on a few more unfortunates. "I'm goin' to get in some other line of work. Best job in this country," he growled testily, "is undertakin'."

Turk pushed on. When he got to the end of the street he started back, still dawdling. He saw Milt Hicks coming down the walk, saw him jawing with Cullum. Saw old Ridge wiping off his talcum box and Hicks, climbing the steps, follow Cullum inside.

Turk cut left behind the Mercantile. He stopped and stood listening for a couple of minutes among the discarded tins and broken crates. He didn't guess anyone was following him but he waited a bit longer just to play double safe. Then he went on toward the rear of Jack Dahl's, scanning the oaks that grew behind the place carefully.

When he got about four doors from them he began catching glimpses of the pole corral. He saw a flash of coffee color through the branches which he took to be High Sailin; and afterwards saw the buckskin, which was the bleached-out shade of coffee with a mess of cream in it. There were eight or ten other horses in the pen with them. He didn't see any guards hanging around.

He began to feel a little more hopeful. If they'd been watching the horses ever since he'd been in bed with that wound they must be pretty well fed up with it. Even taking their turns at it, and if only for the last few days, they'd by this time be looking on the whole deal as crackpot. Nobody but Jake had ever seemed to give a damn if he was with them or not; even downing two men in that street fight with Roman 4 wasn't going to make the bulk of Bill's outfit take him serious. Turk remembered that Tex had said there weren't any of them allowed to quit the mesa right now, but not even this could dampen his sudden rise in spirits. He had a hunch he was going to bring this off.

With this pen full of stock he'd have no trouble mounting Holly. Probably be plenty of saddles around; anyway he and Rita could do without hulls if they had to.

He was just a shade uneasy about how Rita might react to having Holly along, but he didn't see how he could just plain up and leave her. He reckoned he owed her at least the chance to get away.

Some remote part of his thinking suggested she might not be finding time so heavy on her hands here, but he brushed that notion aside with contempt. She was here because she couldn't help herself. Maybe she had kind of led Bill on, making the most of what chances she had. He didn't see how a man could honestly hold that against her, everything considered and Ruebusch being dead and all. There was a cold streak of practicality running through Holly, but she'd pile out of here quick enough once she saw the way.

His blood began to warm as his thoughts swung back to Rita. There, by God, was a girl a man could tie to, and he was glad at long last he'd gathered sense enough to know it. The thoughts of coming home to her would give a man plenty of peck to get on with. You couldn't judge the whole world by what you found around Tombstone. There were other, better places. Someplace he'd find a country both of them could fit into. He'd put his wages into cattle . . .

The sight of Joe Hill jerked his mind away from his thinking. There was a rifle in the crook of Hill's arm. He seemed to be lounging against a tree half asleep but he was doing it where he could watch the corral and Turk knew he would have to take care of Hill first. He spent another three minutes trying to turn up a Clanton before, deciding there wasn't any Clantons around, he commenced injuning up to the tree Hill was propping.

He was reaching for his pistol, getting ready to jump, when Ike Clanton said from out of the branches, "Just unbuckle the belt, boy, an' let that thing drop."

# FOURTEEN

IT WAS HARD—damnably hard, but Turk did it. He didn't have any choice, knowing Ike would be covering him and that a gunshot, even if it didn't out-and-stop him, would fetch the rest of them running before he could ever expect to loose the horses. His time would come, he thought. Better to play along for now and let these galoots think they had the upper hand on him.

They did have, too. Hill came away from the tree, chuckling; and back of Turk, as Turk's gun-weighted belt hit the ground, Jake Gauze laughed nastily. Then the others moved up and were suddenly all about him, sneering and snickering as Hill, waving Turk back, picked his belt up.

Bill said, "Boy, I'm surprised at you."

He didn't look surprised though. He looked like a cat with a mouthful of goldfish.

Turk, having nothing to say, kept his jaws shut.

Bill beckoned Charlie Snow up. Still considering Turk, he said, "Ain't no use in you latherin' about McConaghey's kid—nor about them two girls. They ain't over there. Holly come her

165

ownself and told me what you was up to no sooner than Willbrandt got out of sight."

He grinned at the look of Turk. A couple others snickered.

Turk was lost in the chaos of conflicting thoughts, unable to believe it. The blood roared in his ears. His fists clenched so tight the nails bit into his palms and he was seized with an impulse to smash them into Bill's face. Snow, narrowly watching him, dug the barrel of his pistol into Turk's ribs. He said, "Gawd, what a sucker!" plainly hoping Turk would try something.

Turk had sense enough to know it. The pent-up needs in him turned him giddy. Bill wavered in his vision like something seen through red mist. It got worse when he thought of Rita, but he was helpless and knew it.

He shook his head to clear it and Bill's face came into focus. Bill's dimples were still showing and a reflection of the mocking grin still rode the stiff set of his heavy lips, but there was no mirth in his glance—nothing but the cold black shine of his anger.

"How far'd you figure I was goin' to let you go?"

"I wasn't thinkin' of you," Turk said; and Bill snorted.

"Git his horse," he told Gauze, "an' tie him into the saddle. Hicks—go help Ike and Hill git them grub sacks from Kelly. We're pullin' out right away. John," he growled at Ringo, "you go after Tex and git him roped onto a horse same's the kid here. Zwing, you go pass the word to the rest of the boys. I want every man packin' a—"

166

He never got to the end of that sentence. A shout went up in the road out front. A racket of boots and cursing swept tumultuously nearer through the gut of the passage between Dahl's place and the next to the left of it. For these shreds of split seconds the gang's attention was divided.

Turk didn't wait for anything better. Slamming around in the midst of this uproar he clouted Snow's pistol away from his ribs, hearing a yell as flame burst from its muzzle. He twisted the weapon out of Snow's grasp and struck Snow across the face with the butt of it. As the man reeled back, taking two others with him, Turk crashed a boot at another man's shin and, coming full around, buried his gun-weighted fist in Jake's stomach.

The very fury of his attack held them stunned for a moment. Air left Gauze like the gust from a bellows and as he came doubling over Turk cracked him across the head with the pistol. Turk kneed another as Gauze went down.

Turk reversed the gun and slashed with its barrel. Clanton, trying to leap clear, got hung up in his spurs. Bill's bull-throated roar sailed above the shouts and cursing and Turk, alerted, saw Bill's gun coming up. He lost his advantage trying to duck away from it, crashing into a man whose arms locked about him like the jaws of a vice. He still had his gun free but he couldn't shoot Bill. He stamped sharp heels viciously onto the booted toes of the man who held him, hopes soaring again as the fellow's arms fell away; but the chance was gone. He saw Bill's face springing toward him, saw the gleam of Bill's upswung gun slashing down. He tried to twist away but hands caught him and held him and blackness enveloped him in a bright blaze of rockets.

He didn't see Rita tear out of the alley and crash full tilt into the arms of Zwing Hunt. He didn't know Jake Gauze kicked him twice in the face or that Charlie Snow, staggering over, would have killed him out of hand if Bill hadn't stopped him. He didn't know another thing till he came groggily back to full miserable consciousness nearly an hour later to see the ground reeling under him and realize he was roped face down across a horse.

The dust kicked up by other horses almost strangled him. Every jolting stride of the animal beneath him went like a slap of a hand through his head and he was sick, vomiting wretchedly.

He must have mercifully blanked out again. The next time he opened his eyes it was night and he was stretched on the ground with his wrists lashed behind him and both ankles tied together with rope. He didn't realize this until he tried unsuccessfully to roll over. Pain splintered through cramped arms and legs with the effort. His head and face commenced to throb and he could hardly breathe. His stomach muscles, bruised from contact with the saddle, sorely knotted but the convulsion did not bring anything up. He guessed there was nothing left to bring up.

His face felt as though a horse had lain down on it and his thickened tongue found gaps in his jaw teeth. He thought his head must surely burst and it took him a considerable while to understand the claret lacings of light permeating the blackness came not from the expanding and contraction of his skull but from the flicker and flames of an open fire. It was after this he realized the top half of him was soaking wet.

He heard the growl of Bill's voice tell someone to "git the ropes off him," and felt boots approach and rough hands pulling him over. The pain set him crazy when the loosened ropes let the blood pound through his limbs again; and he groaned, trying to writhe away from it.

"You ain't hurt," Bill said. "You got off damn cheap. Sit up there now and put your mind on what I'm sayin'."

Turk's hands wouldn't hold the weight of him. He dropped back, helpless, on his face and chest and somebody, cursing, pulled him over and, catching him under the arms, dragged him back about ten feet and propped him up against a tree. Zwing Hunt said, "You want me to give him another drenchin'?"

Bill said, "Git away from him. He ain't goin' no-place in that shape."

Turk's head began to clear, but getting it off the ground did little to relieve the splitting ache and throbbing pound of it. He had to hold it still in order to keep his stomach quiet.

His eyes began to function again and he saw Curly Bill and Jake Gauze's squatty shape and, back of them, others of the gang hunkered down around the fire among the gear and blankets that lay scattered about. He couldn't make out Bill's expression with the flames behind him that way.

Jake, farther over, was turned enough that half of his face was lit up by the glow. The venom in his glowering stare leaped against Turk like the glint of a razor.

Bill said, coming nearer, "You got one chance to set yourself straight with this bunch. One chance. We're goin' down to Mexico. You'll be helpin' Jake crack a bank when we git there."

Turk couldn't laugh because his face hurt too bad. He managed a croaking sound though and Bill got the drift. He hunched burly shoulders and cracked his knuckles, saying thinly, "You'll go through with it, kid. Take a look to the left of you."

Turk wasn't minded to give them any satisfaction, but curiosity finally turned his head and the shock of what he saw all but paralyzed his thinking. Rita, heartlessly trussed as a calf for the branding, lay motionless huddled a few feet away from him. Holly's dress, ravaged but still around her, more resembled a dishrag than anything better. The bedraggled hem of its skirt was above her shapely knees and there was dirt ground into them; one sleeve was torn away from the shoulder and a dark bruise showed above the swell of her breast. He saw dried blood on her cheeks and though her eyes were open they were like glass doors in an empty house.

"She's all right," Bill said. "Been handled a little rough is all. How much more of it she gits will be strictly up to you."

Turk's rigid face was the color of a wagon sheet. Now that the first awful sickness had passed, the stunned incredulity that had held him silent was loosening its hold and a black rage was pounding through him, a towering monstrous fury the like of which he'd never known. He sat there shaking like a man with the ague but this was not the kid who had been duped at Willow Springs.

He got hold of himself. "I'm listenin'," he said finally.

Bill chuckled, throwing a look at Jake Gauze. "You can take them ropes off Willbrandt now." He brought his glance back to Turk.

"Here's the deal. I'm takin' the most of the boys down to Matamoros—everything's set. At Mier we split up. Jake will take ten men, includin' you and Willbrandt, to Monterrey. One of the banks there will be holding fifty thousand in U.S. dollars—payrolls fer gringo mines. You'll pull the stickup and keep the bank crowd under gunpoint while Hughes and Tex Willbrandt is sackin' up the dough. The rest of the boys, with Jake, will be holdin' the horses and keepin' things quiet outside. It's a pushover—Jake'll give you the details later. We'll wait fer you at Hyler's Pass. Rita stays with us."

He didn't make any remarks about what would happen to her if Turk or Willbrandt fouled up the bank job. He didn't have to.

They reached Guerrero ten days later. It was a gruelling trip and they were all saddle gaunted and the horses needed a rest. Bill used nothing but the best but they were in hard shape. Bill decided to spend three days around the place, where he would pose as a Texas cow boss on his way to

Villaldama. But Jake Gauze said to hell with the rest, his boys would take the trail to Monterrey come daybreak. Bill, grinning, struck off for the town with Ringo and Ike Clanton while the rest of the outfit offsaddled and those appointed to the task commenced preparations for supper.

Turk saw Rita being untied to help with this but he was sent by Hughes to hunt for wood or cow chips and did not get to speak with her. She'd been kept away from him during the rides and there had so far been little chance at their camps for him to do much more than speak a few brief words of reassurance to her. There were galled places and several running sores where her ankles had been roped each day to the fishcord cinch underneath her horse's belly, and she looked gaunt and utterly hopeless. There was a volcano of resentment building up inside of Turk but there'd been nothing he could do about it. Nor had he been able to talk with Willbrandt. The three of them were under constant watch and Turk had done what he'd been told to do and kept his mouth tight buttoned lest things be made more difficult for her. But he was storing it up.

He made three trips to the fire with his towsack full of cow chips before he could get a word with her. Billy Grounds was peeling spuds but Hughes called him off for something before Turk got there. It left the girl briefly alone with him.

She plainly meant to ignore him but the second time he spoke her name it brought her head around. She stared, unwilling to look at him, off across to where Hughes stood talking with

172

Grounds. Turk said, "I'll make this up to you, Rita."

"It doesn't matter."

"Of course it matters!"

"Nothing matters any more," she said listlessly. "I'll soon be dead."

The resigned indifference of her tone both shocked and angered him. "Don't talk like that!" he said sharply. "I've been pretty much of a fool, but soon's I git back from this Monterrey thing—"

"You won't be coming back," she said harshly. "When you've done what they want Jake will kill you."

"He may try but I'll be back. You can count on it."

Her eyes touched his face. There was life in them now. He was reminded of the look sometimes seen on a prodded bull. "Why do you keep talking about it? You don't have to pretend you are interested—I don't want your pity." She said with a look almost of hate on her features, "Go back to your ripe wheat woman if you get free— she has had more experience, she will know how to please you!"

Turk's ears were hot and the blood was pounding in his throat but he was going to have his say if he had to grab and hold her. He did reach out but she eluded his grasp. There was plenty of fire in her now. Her eyes blazed at him.

Turk's voice was bitter but it was stubborn too. "You got a right to them thoughts, a heap more right than you know, I reckon, but when I git back I'm comin' for you. No matter where you are I'm

173

going to find you. And we're going to find a priest and git the right words said, words that'll bind you and me together forever—"

"Forever," Hughes said, coming up with his gun out, "is the hole you're bein' dumped into if you don't pick up that sack and get back to your dung huntin' pronto."

# FIFTEEN

IT WAS LONG after dark and they had two fires going and most of the bunch had eaten and were scattered around, some working over their gear, some cleaning their guns and some sleeping, when Curly Bill, Ringo and the rawboned Clanton got back from town. Bill's mouth was tight and his eyes looked ugly. "Put out them fires and saddle up," he shouted.

"What's the big idea?" Hughes said. "I thought—"

"We're gittin' out of here. On the double!"

It developed that Guerrero had been packed to the gills with Mexican vaqueros holding some kind of a celebration. At first everything had gone smooth as silk. Bill had bought his supplies and a couple dozen extra saddle horses and the three had gone into a saloon for some refreshment. The local *patron*—a big rancher and his burly cow boss had been in there and these and John Ringo had got into a card game. Clanton and Bill had been at the bar drinking. When Bill left to find a man with a wagon to fetch out the grub he'd bought,

175

Clanton had been making passes at a Mexican bar maid. The girl's husband had come in but Ike had tentatively smoothed things over when sharp words arose at the card table. The burly Mexican cow boss had accused Ringo of dealing off the bottom of the deck. Bill was coming in the door when Ringo jumped up and shot the man. Nothing after that seemed to Turk to be very coherent, but before the three had got out of there there were four dead Mexicans sprawled on the floor, and one of them was the old don himself.

"Hell," Jake Gauze scoffed, "We can take care of a bunch of dumb cow hands—"

"We can't afford a fight now," Bill snarled, "we've got to git whackin'. That goddam cow boss has sent for the *Rurales.*"

There was no more argument. The fires were doused and ten minutes later they were all in leather, riding. Nobody cared to invite gunplay with the Mexican mounted police who had a hard reputation and were recruited mostly from outlaws. Win, lose or draw, Bill's whole outfit knew that if they tangled with *Rurales* their bank and other plans were done for. They rode straight west on the trail to Paras. "We'll swing around it," Bill said, "and drop south to Agualeguas. We'll git into the hills and lose those bastards before we do anything else—we kin rest later."

The horses were staggering when they got into the hills, but they did get into them; and if they had not lost the vaqueros from Guerrero, at least they had seen no evidence of their proximity—nor did they now. Bill ordered the gang down for a two-hour rest.

In the rush of getting away from Guerrero there'd been no chance to pick up the supplies Bill had bought or the horses. Tempers were short. Bill and Ringo weren't speaking. In the milky half light that was forerunner to dawn Bill was just making ready to call in the pickets when a sudden eruption of cursing broke out, terminated by the loud crash of gunshots.

Bill came through the gray gloom like the wrath of God. Zwing Hunt was down with a bullet through his groin and Milt Hicks stood over him with a pistol in his fist, daring Grounds to take a hand in it. Hunt, it seemed, had been discovered by Hicks sneaking grub from what was left of the outfit's scanty rations.

"You damn fools!" Bill snarled, sending Grounds reeling with a blow to the jaw. "Git into your saddles!" He waved his arms, including all of them. "Next sonofabitch pops a cap around here better put one into himself or by Gawd I'll do it for him!"

The pickets came in, drawn by the gunfire; and Charlie Snow, as the others moved off to catch up their horses, complained that Turk ought to be tied lest, during the day's run through these timbered hills, he try to get away from them. "Hell with that," Bill growled, still glaring at Hicks, "he ain't like to try nothin' long's we've got that damn girl." He shoved Snow aside and went tramping after his horse.

Turk hadn't even been thinking of flight but now looking up, he crossed glances with Willbrandt and saw the man's eyebrows lift. Turk threw the gear on High Sailin, remembering that Rita was riding the tough buckskin and that, in the confusion of quitting their last camp, Hughes had neglected to re-rope her ankles.

They moved south through the rolling hills at a dog-trot. The sun came up and fell hot and strong on Turk's left side and shoulder. But after a couple of hours it hazed over.

The terrain became more difficult. Their pace was slowed to a walk and Turk, still considering Willbrandt's show of raised eyebrows, reckoned thoughts of escape were exercising him too. They had little to look forward to, either of them—Rita was right about that. He'd seen enough of Bill's methods to know that once Bill's purpose was served and the gang had grabbed that bank dough, there would be no gnashing of teeth or wailing if Jake's crew came back with two empty saddles.

Jake had taken a dislike to Turk right from the start. And the guy was plumb crazy—mean and ornery was the way Rita had put it; completely no good, a renegade who had caused his family nothing but grief. A kill-crazy chaparral wolf. Look at the way he used his own sister—his half-sister really, but still blood of his blood. Never opening his mouth no matter how this bunch treated her.

An hour short of noon Bill called another halt to rest and graze the horses. They were in a cup-shaped valley ringed by open hills. The air was heavy, stifling. Bill sent three men up the slope to watch their backtrail. Jerked beef was passed around, salty and thirst-inspiring. Fortunately there was water. Willbrandt sat with legs stretched out, his back against the hot slant of a boulder. Gauze motioned Turk over beside him and left Charlie Snow to stretch the saddle cramp out of their backs, but the most of the bunch simply sprawled in the grass, hats over their faces, catching what rest they were able.

Willbrandt said, "You better get that girl outa here. I don't cotton to the way that damn Grounds has been eyin' her."

Turk said, "Tonight?"

They'd been keeping it low, not even looking toward each other. Before Willbrandt could answer, Snow came catfooting over with a scowl and told them to shut their damned faces. He was spoiling for trouble, just looking for an excuse to work them over with his six-shooter.

Turk let the talk go, chewing down on his temper, but Willbrandt said, "You been noticing that sky?"

Snow swelled up like a poised pup, anger darkening the wrinkled skin above his collar. He stepped nearer to Willbrandt, yanking out his gun like he was minded to shut Tex's mouth himself. Just short of hitting him something stayed Snow's hand. "Get around the other side of that rock," he snarled. "You open your trap again to me and I'll give you something to sing about!"

Willbrandt got up with a shrug and moved around to the rock's other side, settling down again. He tipped the slant of his hat across his eyes. Something about the gesture infuriated Snow. Sucking air into his lungs he shouted for Billy Grounds and Joe Hill.

The two came running. "Grab that bastard and

haul him up where I kin get at him!" Snow yelled hoarsely, snatching his belt off. Turk, watching the pair closing in on Tex, thrust a boot out and sent Grounds sprawling. Snow spun, cursing, as Turk jumped to his feet; he tried to catch Turk in the face with the buckle of that belt, but Turk put up his arm, diving under it, his other fist connecting solidly with Snow's jaw. Snow let go of the belt and let his head roll, afterwards leaping at Turk with a switch knife. Turk grabbed off his hat and threw it at the man. Before he could do anything else, or Snow could grab him, a big fist grabbed Turk and whirled him crashing into the boulder. There was a bone-bruising thud of flesh against flesh, a gasping whistle of breath, and Snow went by like the westbound express. Ringo, Jake Gauze and four or five others stood near enough to have grabbed him but no one put out a hand. He struck the trampled-down grass all spraddled out and got up, visibly shaking, with his face like putty.

"I ain't tellin' you fools again!" Bill roared. "That's dust back yonder! Pile into them saddles!"

The bunch took one look and ran for their horses. In the resultant confusion, Turk, pushing himself off the rock with skinned hands, caught a glint in the grass, reeled a few groggy steps and stumbled, falling across it. It was a gun, all right. He got it into his shirtfront and shoved to his feet. Tex, crossing in front of him, muttered, "Somethin' you oughta know. That bank—"

"Git whackin'!" Gauze shouted, whirling around and scowling back at them.

180

They pushed steadily into the hot winds from the south. Their sore-footed, dust raddled, dog-weary horses were still moving three hours later, but they were strung out now for half a mile and some of them weren't going to last much longer. The faces of the men were getting desperate, Turk saw, as they looked back across their shoulders. That dust Bill had spotted was drawing perceptibly nearer and was obviously whipped up by a large body of horsemen which no one doubted were *Rurales* reinforced by the dead don's vaqueros.

Bill pulled up, twisting around in his saddle, shoulders bulking sharp against the queer lemon look of the sky. "We're goin' to have to split up. Jake's boys will meet at Higueras—I'll look for my bunch outside Aldamas. Mebbe we can lose those bastards in this storm. Five-six of you bust off into the east with Clanton. Some more of you go with Hughes—John, here, will take a few. Rest of you foller me. Let's go!"

The wind fell as dust whirled around them. Horses flattened their ears under the bite of spurs and flogging squirts as the gang streaked off in six directions. Some were bound to see gunsmoke but, equally certain, some of them, at least, would get clean away. It was the only chance they had with tired mounts. Turk tried to see which bunch Rita was wrapped up in but in that pounding bedlam of dust and confusion he could not find her. Charlie Snow came pelting astride his blue roan and struck High Sailin across the rump with his quirt and Milt Hicks came up behind him, hazing Turk after Jake. There was no chance of Turk getting out of it.

They ran down a ridge and quartered south again, belaboring their mounts through a rock littered gulch that, after two miles, opened into another pass between hills; and the wind struck them, cooler. There were six of them with Jake and Turk saw Willbrandt pounding along beside Gauze up in front.

They cut into another canyon and they were climbing through spruce and juniper. The country was getting rougher and darkness was closing in on them with the wind getting colder and colder. Coming out on ledgerock at the top of the grade Turk saw that the ones ahead of him had pulled up. Jake said, "There's two ways we kin go here," and pointed. "Down there, which is shorter and open, or off to the left up into them slopes where there's cover when we git to it."

Snow said, "You're bossin' this," and Jake twisted his mouth at him. "We swing left then," he said, "an' be damn sure you remember it."

He led off, Willbrandt following; and then Turk saw Rita. She was trying to get back to him but Hicks turned in front of her, blocking the trail, grinning, forcing her on again. There was a lift of gladness in Turk, then flaring anger at Hicks overshadowed by a frustrating sense of futility. He still had the gun but he knew better than to reach for it. The watchful shine of these men's glances curled around him like a wall of knives, hemming him in with their distrust and with their readiness for violence. It was like the stench rolling off a swamp—that plain. Shivering, he glanced again at the sky; and back of him Grounds said, "Don't take root there!"

He kneed High Sailin after the others, following the rumps of their horses through the failing light, dogging them around the ribs of towering rocks and between the gray faces of balanced boulders that hugged the trail like crouching cats; and the raw wind beat against him, flapping the brim of his hat and his scarf ends.

Bill in his shrewdness had tied Turk's hands with his unvoiced threat against Rita, but that was past. Now they were both with Jake; and Turk, in Jake's scheme of things, was expendable. Jake would kill him out of hand on the thinnest pretense of an excuse. There was no need to ask where that would leave Rita. There was nothing Turk could do but play along.

They came onto a high plateau in the first full tide of a too early darkness with storm streaks flogging the tops of the grass roots and a hard wind roaring up out of the south. He had seen bad storms around Tombstone but never anything to compare with the look of the one building now. They crossed the spine of the bench with dust and flung grit pelting into their faces. Turk had to button his brush jacket to keep it from being ripped off him. Then, as they hit the far end of this open, the wind quit abruptly. It became so still he got to wondering if his ears were stopped up, but the others also were staring strangely about them. In this eerie light objects even at some distance appeared as sharply defined as though bathed in fluorescence. "Be a dinger," Willbrandt grunted, drawing black looks from those who rode nearest him.

Gauze turned his horse up the bleak slope ahead of them, still scowling into the south where, pale against the far horizon, there was what looked to be a considerable stretch of sand. Turk wondered what was gnawing him.

He found it hard to reconcile this dour killer with his relationship to Rita. He got to thinking inexplicably of what Willbrandt had been saying when Snow had broken their talk up. "That bank—" Tex had said, obviously attempting to get something across to him. Turk had a hunch it had been something important or Snow wouldn't have come tearing into them so rabidly. Turk was minded to try to come up with Tex now . . .

He waited out the climb till they came onto another grassy bench—this whole region was like that, tiny prairies locked between broken country and timber. They were high enough now to get a fairly wide view of it. Some of those stretches looked pretty ugly, not the kind of terrain a man would care to prowl come nightfall. But now, as his stare again touched that south horizon, he ceased to wonder at Jake's frowning looks. What he had taken for sand covered a greater area now. It was nearer, more like fog, a kind of lemonish dun in appearance, rough and wavery as though filled with movement and ragged along the high top edge like the mane of a horse with the wind streaming through it. *Dust!*

It was coming straight for them. It was still at a considerable distance but it was covering ground with an astonishing speed. Turk nudged High

Sailin's ribs with a spur, putting the horse around Milt Hicks and easing him forward toward the girl's position.

Snow called after him but Turk ignored it. Shrugging out of his brush jacket he maneuvered the brown alongside the girl's buckskin. "Here . . . git into this," he said, holding it out to her.

She accepted it, smiling shyly; but her eyes as she buttoned it about her were solemn. Jake glanced back wtihout speaking, hardly noticing, and almost at once his frowning stare returned to that towering onsweeping wall of dust. It was nearer, perceptibly nearer, Turk saw with a mounting excitement. If, as seemed likely, it should shortly envelop them . . .

He tried to catch Willbrandt's eye where he rode beyond the girl. But Rita, crowding the buckskin against High Sailin, leaned toward Turk, saying desperately, "We've simply got to do something. That bank—"

"Watch it!" Willbrandt growled.

Reflex put Turk's spur into the brown and the murderous sweep of Snow's swinging rifle butt, thus deprived of its goal, almost tore Snow out of the stirrups. Turk drove High Sailin hard at Snow's roan but Willbrandt's arm, catching Turk around the middle, dragged him bodily from the saddle. "Wait, you fool—wait for the dust!" Tex breathed.

Snow wasn't waiting for anything. He slammed his horse into Willbrandt's mount pinning Turk, still caught in the circle of Tex's arm, between them. Twice Snow's sledging knuckles crashed into Turk's face before Turk, going limp, dropped into a maelstrom of churning hoofs. He heard Rita scream and was still enough conscious to cover his head with his arms, but he was struck three times before those hoofs cleared away from him.

It looked worse than it was because, in spite of the blood, in such close quarters the horses hadn't chance to put much heart behind their kicking.

A rough hand caught Turk's shoulder and hauled him upright. Milt Hicks this was, he noticed, and saw Rita running toward him. Snow's shape cut in between them and he saw Snow's fist coming at him again. He let his head roll with the blow but it was still bad enough. Snow's left hand got a hold on Turk's shirtfront and his right went back to full cock for another. More by instinct than anything Turk brought up a knee and Snow reeled away from him.

Hicks tightened his grip. "Grounds—" Jake yelled, "work him over with your pistol!"

Hicks had both of Turk's arms twisted back of him and things were happening so fast they hadn't yet had time to realize Turk was making his final stand. Snow was still doubled over, hugging himself, whimpering. Turk tried to ward off Grounds with an outthrust leg but Hicks kicked the other leg out from under him. Turk's whole sagged weight wasn't enough to buckle Hicks; but Rita was into it now, pounding Hicks and clawing at him.

If Willbrandt had sided with them they might have had a chance, but the rusty-haired peppermint-chewer remained wedded to his saddle with his gray cheeks strictly neutral.

As Grounds came leaping in Turk hauled up

both knees and slammed booted heels down, hoping to connect with Hick's instep. Hicks was watching for it and shifted but Turk managed to put him off balance. He tried in the interim to get at Hick's holster and Hicks, trying to block that, tripped under Rita's pummeling.

They went down, Turk taking the brunt of it. But Hick's hold was loosened. Turk wrenched one arm free and dug in his heels, twisting with all the strength that was in him. It forced Hicks over, giving Turk a chance to pull some air into his lungs. Wind scoured his cheeks with grit and he heard the increasing fury of it howl across the bench. He scratched Hick's legs with his blunt-roweled spurs, writhing, struggling to break clear of the man. He flipped over, pounding his free fist into Hick's belly, and Hicks came back with shortarm jabs to the jaw. Turk, shifting again, saw Jake piling out of his saddle, face twisted with rage and impatience. "Get in there, Grounds, an' smash him!"

Grounds tried. Turk lashed out with a leg, the sharp toe of his boot catching Grounds in the knee. Grounds yelled, dropping back. Rita, with both hands clenched in Hick's hair, was beating Hicks' head against the shale littered earth. Willbrandt's jaded horse began pitching, getting into Jake's way as Jake snatched out his pistol.

Grounds was circling again. Snow, making sounds like a busted accordion, was on hands and knees trying to locate his six-shooter. Grounds, ready now, was coming in low with a lifted gun, plainly bent on cracking Turk's skull. Turk got loose of Hick's hold just as Grounds made his swing and that down-flailing gun barrel, barely missing Turk's head, buried its steel in Hick's throat with the sound of a cow coming out a bog hole.

Rita, letting go of Hicks' head, jumped up just as Turk gained his feet. He thrust her away from him. "Git your horse!" he gasped, flinging himself to the left as Grounds, recovering, fired. Another gun hammered back at Turk. He felt the slug break flesh along his right thigh and, wincing away from it, lost his balance. He went down, almost falling into the flame of Ground's gun, the powderblast half blinding him. He lurched erect, coughing, trying to get the picked-up pistol from the tatters of his shirt.

Strange, he thought, what pranks a man's mind played. Once he'd have given his right arm to ride with this bunch; now all he wanted was Rita and a chance to get out of this. He saw Grounds, through the drifting dust, desperately cramming his gun with fresh loads.

Turk had the pistol clear of his shirt now and lifted it. But that was immature, the Curly Bill way. While he stood hesitating, torn between a natural desire and the new hard-won knowledge of a man's responsibilities, dust came with a howling gust of wind, enveloping the bench, absorbing sound, blotting everything from sight.

He ran, filled with fright, calling Rita's name; and the wind took hold of him, buffeting and staggering him, suffocating as a blanket, fencing him in with his terror of losing her.

Like a ghost out of nowhere she appeared on High Sailin, kicked a foot from the stirrup and reached down a hand for him. Shaking with reaction he got a boot in the oxbow, was about to swing up, when a second mounted shape appeared through the murk. Barely discernible, it was bucking the teeth of the wind, pushing south at the very edge of visibility, perhaps thirty feet to the right of them.

Convinced it was Willbrandt, Turk cried out, shouting hoarsely. Catching hold of the brown's reins he was about to go plunging after the man when three coronas of light briefly blossomed through the dust. It was the tiny cork-stopper popping of gunfire that sent Turk up behind Rita and hammered his heels into High Sailin's flanks.

Twice within the hour Turk wanted to stop and rest the horse, but both times the girl's desperate voice kept them going. "Now," she said abruptly, "here there is a cave where we can take shelter for a little while."

"How come you know about it?"

"It is not far from Monterrey—all my life I have ridden these hills. Inside it will be dry and there'll be wood. We'll have a fire. A little one."

"But won't Jake . . . ?"

"Hoh! He will never find this place; but we must not stay. We dare not chance that he shall reach the town before us. We must warn the garrison what he plans. My poor father's small life savings are in that bank. For him it would be ruin— You think this is perhaps too much I ask? To pay for our great happiness?"

His arm gripped her waist more tightly. Nothing would ever be too much for that. The soldiers might not catch Bill's bunch, but other soldiers, elsewhere, probably would before Bill was done with this. Turk wondered if Holly would be with him then. Probably not, for Bill was not the kind, Turk knew now, who could long be true to anyone. Or to anything but the wildness in him. But she'd make out; there would always be another man somewhere.

"No," Turk said, "we must let them know about Jake, of course. We'll push straight on. After we're married—"

"Ah, *querido*—heart of my heart . . ." Twisting around she pressed her cold cheek to his, and there was warmness between them. "We will do this thing then. And all I will care for after that— all I will care to be, I mean, is wife to a cowman. To you, Turkey Red!"

**Nelson Nye** was born in Chicago, Illinois. He was educated in schools in Ohio and Massachusetts and attended the Cincinnati Art Academy. His early journalism experience was writing publicity releases and book reviews for the *Cincinnati Times-Star* and the *Buffalo Evening News*. In 1935 he began working as a ranch hand in Texas and California and became an expert on breeding quarter horses on his own ranch outside Tucson, Arizona. Much of this love for horses can be found in exceptional novels such as *Wild Horse Shorty* and *Blood of Kings*. He published his first Western short story in *Thrilling Western* and his first Western novel in 1936. He continued from then on to write prolifically, both under his own name and the bylines Drake C. Denver and Clem Colt. During the Second World War, he served with the U.S. Army Field Artillery. In 1949–1952 he worked as horse editor for *Texas Livestock Journal.* He was one of the founding members of the Western Writers of America in 1953 and served twice as its president. His first Golden Spur Award from the Western Writers of America came to him for best Western reviewer and critic in 1954. In 1958–1962 he was frontier fiction reviewer for the *New York Times Book Review.* His second Golden Spur came for his novel *Long Run*. His virtues as an author of Western fiction include a tremendous sense of authenticity, an ability to keep the pace of a story from ever lagging, and a fecund inventiveness for plot twists and situations. Some of his finest novels have had off-trail protagonists such as *The Barber of Tubac,* and both *Not Grass Alone* and *Strawberry Roan* are notable for their outstanding female characters. His books have sold over 50,000,000 copies worldwide and have been translated into the principal European languages. The *Los Angeles Times* once praised him for his "marvelous lingo, salty humor, and real characters." Above all, a Nye Western possesses a vital energy that is both propulsive and persuasive.